BEHIND THE WIND

Wirrun was happy. He was living free with his golden
girl Murra, and they took what they needed from the
land as men used to do. But Murra, laughing, lovely
Murra, had once been Yunggamurra, a water spirit,
and she knew that one day her sisters would come to
claim her back.

Meanwhile another threat was lurking in dark
corners of the land, growing in power; an evil and mysterious thing that called itself death. It was a man's
creation, though it had gone awry, and Wirrun was
called on to set it right.

So the shadows closed about Wirrun as he went to
seek out death, to bind it or be destroyed by it.

The previous books in this trilogy, *The Ice is Coming*
and *The Dark Bright Water*, are also available in Puffin
Plus.

THE BOOK OF WIRRUN

Behind the Wind

Patricia Wrightson

PUFFIN BOOKS

Puffin Books, Penguin Books Australia Ltd,
487 Maroondah Highway, P.O. Box 257
Ringwood, Victoria, 3134, Australia
Penguin Books Ltd,
Harmondsworth, Middlesex, England
Penguin Books,
40 West 23rd Street, New York, N.Y. 10010, U.S.A.
Penguin Books Canada Ltd,
2801 John Street, Markham, Ontario, Canada
Penguin Books (N.Z.) Ltd,
182-190 Wairau Road, Auckland 10, New Zealand

First published by Hutchinson Junior Books Ltd, 1981
Published by Penguin Books Australia, 1983
Copyright © Patricia Wrightson, 1981

Offset from the Hutchinson hardback edition
Made and printed in Australia by
Dominion Press Hedges & Bell

CIP

Wrightson, Patricia.
Behind the wind.

First published: Richmond, Vic: Hutchinson of
Australia, 1981.
For adolescents.
ISBN 0 14 031629 9.

I. Title.

A823'.3

Contents

Author's Note

I could not have the temerity to invent the kind of experience
an Aboriginal Australian might have in a meeting with death,
or of such mystical processes as initiation at any of its levels.
In section six of this story Wirrun's experiences with Wulgaru
are heavily based on original accounts collected by Bill Harney
and included in his book *Tales from the Aborigines* (Rigby,
Adelaide). The events I have adapted from his two stories
'Mahlindji's Ride with Wulgaru' and 'How Bema Became a
Doctor'; but for the appearance and characteristics of the
monster I have adhered to first records as given in the story
'How Djarapa Made Wulgaru'.

Behind
the Wind

Wind Ride
The Wide Water
Jimmy Ginger's Country
Merv Bula's Country
Rainforest
Wind Ride
Jug Ride
Plateau Country
Fire Country
Ularra's Country
Pungalonga Ride
Jambun Ride
Frog-Woman's Ride
Country of Noatch

ONE

A Thing with no Body

I

It was early autumn when Jimmy Ginger went after prawns. Far away down the world the ice-winds had begun to probe at the southern coast, and in the tropic north the Wet had dwindled into a few sharp storms. The brassy sun was softening into gold but the warm sea held the memory of summer. All down the long east coast of the old south land the white race of Happy Folk still swam or ate ice-cream and drank from frosty cans, while the sun toasted their white skins as brown as those of the People. The only sign of autumn was a scattering of more leathery tans: Inlanders on holiday too, released from their farms at last. But the Happy Folk knew so little of their white cousins that they did not recognise this as a sign of autumn.

Jimmy belonged to neither of the white-skinned races; his dark brown skin was leathered and tanned almost black. He was one of the People, long in the land before these white men ever saw it or were a race at all. He stayed away from them in shy, sulky pride and did his prawning in the mouth of a creek where mud and mangroves and mosquitoes made the place his own.

Hidden among the mangroves was an old timber boat, his to use when it wasn't wanted. He let his net fall heavily from his shoulder into the boat. It was a pocket-net, with a wide mouth to be tied between two stays and a long narrowing pocket to drift along the tide; small as such nets go, but an awkward weight for one man to handle. Jimmy was used to it, and strong and active for his age; he manhandled the boat between sharp mangrove-roots into open water, pushed off and jumped aboard in one movement, and rowed a little way frowning at the tide. The rusty rowlocks squealed.

In about five feet of water, near but not too near a belt of mangroves, two leaning poles were driven into the deep, soft mud of the bottom. Between them Jimmy tied his net by the ropes at its mouth, leaving enough slack to allow for the fall, and then the rise, of the tide. He sat for a moment watching the capped detergent-bottles that were his floats: seeing in his mind the mouth of the net gaping wide into the tide, the long pocket feeling along the mud. Then he took the oars, rowed back into the mangroves, stepped out and moored the boat.

He went ashore through mangroves and walked up a rise into banksias, above the mud and mosquitoes. He had left his lunch and two cans of beer up there where the honey-eater birds called rudely. To Jimmy a day's fishing or prawning meant a day alone in the bush. He liked company when the time was right: a quiet drink and a game of cards with friends, a night of talk and singing, or to watch young folk bouncing laughter off each other. But now that he was older he liked to come often to the scrub, to let the quiet flow into him and to remember.

He ate bread and cold mutton, drank one can of beer very slowly and left the other to keep cool in a spiky bush of heath. He watched birds and lizards, sang a little to himself in a heavy drone. He lay back under banksias to watch the silver undersides of leaves and the black wicked faces of cones and the blue shine of sky beyond; and in the warm shade he slept.

He woke aware and tingling, rigid except for the hair that lifted and crawled on the back of his neck. Something was near—something bad. He lay still to listen and look.

There was nothing he could see or hear—no snake's rustle or slither, no smoke or crackle of fire, no sound even of birds. Slowly, slowly, he stirred and raised his head: nothing but a grey spider on grey bark. And still every tingling nerve and creeping hair of Jimmy Ginger told him that something bad was near.

And that was very bad, for an unknown evil is one a man

can't guard against. Little by little, head turning and heart bumping, Jimmy sat up—stood—searched quietly near at hand. Nothing. He stood waiting, sure yet now not sure. Some old bad thing had been near, some menace that must have come to him out of the land itself in one of its dark moods. He had lived a long time with the land and the People and knew of things like that; but had it passed?

The colour of the sky between branches told him that the afternoon was going. He must not get trapped in this place by night and there was still his net; the tide would be filling. In a while he wiped his forehead and went to fetch his second can of beer. He needed it now.

It winked out of its bush, still cool enough for Jimmy. He parted the prickly branches with one hand to reach in with the other, grasped the can and saw through parted twigs the grey sandy soil beneath the bush. And the thing was there.

It was nothing that he knew. It had no body. It was just a pair of red-glowing eyes in some dark, rough sort of face. But the eyes looked at Jimmy, looked deep into him before he could move.

He sprang off with a yell and ran: down the slope into the mangroves, stumbling on roots and shoving his feet through risen water. He reached the boat, clambered or fell into it and sat shaking. The mangroves and the shadowed water enclosed him. When he could use his hands he pulled on the rope to bring the boat back to its mooring, fumbled with the knot to untie it, seized the oars and pulled in short hard jabs. When he reached open water he shipped the oars, wrenched open his can of beer and drank.

It had been bad all right, and worse because he didn't know the thing. The old stories told a man what he might see and what he ought to do, and Jimmy knew them. But he'd never heard of a thing like this in his country. He drank and shivered: lucky to be here, in the boat on the water with the old detergent-bottles floating near . . . but night would come and he had to get home.

He finished the beer, dropped the can with a clatter and roused himself to pull to each leaning pole in turn and unfasten his net. Then he began to haul it in. It came heavily, tugging against him; he had to put his mind to it and that was good. When he had it half in the boat, wet and heavy about his legs so that he could hardly move them, he glanced down to free his feet. And again the thing was there . . . lying in the bottom like some horrible crab . . . looking at Jimmy with those red-glowing eyes that he somehow knew a man should never see.

Jimmy gave an old man's hoarse scream and took a hobbled leap—overbalanced with the weight of the net—grabbed at it as he went overboard into deep water. The boat slid hard away into the current. Jimmy struggled and fought with his net while the boat with its shipped oars moved gently off on the tide.

Someone found it two days later stranded on the beach outside the creek, its oars still neatly shipped and an empty beer-can rolling in the bottom. It was a week before they found Jimmy Ginger bobbing in the surf, still tangled in his net.

The newspapers called it another fishing accident and mentioned the beer-can lying in the boat; but the People of that country shook their heads and talked quietly together. The weather had been calm all that week. They had known Jimmy well. He was not a man to drink too much alone, in the scrub or on the water, and not a man to tangle himself in his own fishing gear. The People found his death strange and troubling and told some of the old stories again when they were together at night.

2

Stories of Jimmy's death went from man to man among the
People of his country, and up and down the coast to other
eastern countries of the land. But none of them told of a
thing with no body and with red-glowing penetrating eyes
in a rough unfinished face. Nobody in the countries on that
coast knew of such a thing. In all the east only one other man
saw that face, and he did not speak of it or know of Jimmy
Ginger.

He was a broad-shouldered dark-eyed young man with the
heavy brow and the wide smile of the People. They called
him Wirrun, though he had a white man's name among the
Happy Folk in the town where he had grown up and worked.
Now he had given up towns and jobs and cheap lonely rooms
to live free in the old way with his new wife Murra; or as
near the old way as they could come. They walked where
they chose in the lonely back country and took what the land
gave them of roots and fish and possum; took rabbits in wire
snares that they could always replace from some broken-down
fence; stayed a day by a creek where the fish were good or
the weather called them to swim; and only now and then,
when they might need something that had to be bought with
money, would Wirrun look for an Inlander with a starved
woodheap or a half-painted shed neglected.

Now they were walking a plateau-country under the north-
pointing finger of the Cape; and they travelled east because
Murra was afraid of the west. On the day Jimmy Ginger
went after prawns they had found a deep gorge with a good
creek in it; and it seemed to them both that this warm,

sheltered stillness where the shadows would lie cool in the afternoon was a good place to spend a day and a night. They had set a few snares before they swam in a deep pool of the creek. When they were tired of swimming Wirrun lay and dozed in the sun on the bank while Murra knelt beside him and delicately plastered his head with mud. Her lovely face was sharp with mischief.

Wirrun stirred, and she grew still and alert as a bird. He muttered; turned his head; felt the weight of mud and woke and grabbed. But Murra had sprung away and stood laughing at him. He struggled up wiping trickles of mud from his eyes and pretending to be still stupid with sun and sleep; he knew already that barring accidents he couldn't catch her, but another thing he had learnt was when and how to try.

At the right moment he lunged, shouting "Got you!" But he had only succeeded in closing the distance.

She ran like a shadow, nothing moving under her feet, and he thudded after her, scattering pebbles. She doubled past him to a twisted ti-tree that hung over the creek and sprang at a branch. "Clumsy!" she called in a high sweet voice as she swung into the tree.

He knew what would happen—she would dive and hide in the water and be lost for half an hour. He flung himself at the tree and climbed. He was nearer than Murra had thought. She ran far out along a branch and he followed rashly. The branch sagged, cracked—Murra dived and Wirrun tumbled. The water closed over them both together. The shatter-and-crash of water rang through the gorge with the ringing of their laughter.

The mud was washed from Wirrun's hair.

They came out of the water, Murra bringing a fat catfish for when it should be wanted, and dried themselves again with a ragged towel. Wirrun pulled on his frayed shorts and fastened a belt from which hung a bag of netted twine with a grey-fur bundle inside. Murra drew over her head a man's shirt of knitted cotton, faded blue and long enough to hang past her knees; she lifted her long wet hair free of the neck and shook it.

Dressed, they went to inspect their snares. They had one young rabbit. Murra took it out with a hunter's cry of triumph, stroked the trembling thing with a gentle finger, broke its neck with a sudden quick twist and stood stroking the fur again. It was Wirrun who had taught her how to kill a rabbit quickly and painlessly, but he had to crush an impulse to take it roughly from her hands.

By now there was no sun left in the gorge.

"It'll come dark pretty quick down here," he said. "Do you want to take that poor thing back to the creek? I gotta find wood for a fire."

She nodded and turned back. She was bored by wood and suspicious of fire. Wirrun would light the fire and do the cooking, but she might clean and prepare the catch unless she found some other game to play.

He watched her go and began to hunt for firewood, throwing the pieces he found into a heap from which he could gather them later. There was a dark stand of she-oaks a little way off; fallen branches from those would make a quick, hot fire. He worked towards them.

They were tall old trees standing close, and between them it was already twilight. One of them was dead, half fallen and held in the branches of another. He ripped off long strips of the dead bark to act as a fire-starter and moved around it to look for broken branches. As he passed the torn-out roots he thought something glowed among them and bent to look.

Red-glowing eyes looked back.

Wirrun's face darkened and he stood up quickly. His hand had flown to the net bag at his belt. In a moment, still gripping the bag, he bent among fallen strips of bark and looked again.

The eyes looked back, knowing and menacing. There was no body. The clumsy face lay pressed against the soil.

Wirrun felt through his veins a flare of angry hate. He

felt in his palm the roughness of the netted bag, and inside
it the soft winding of possum-fur cord, and inside that the
hardness of stone and the stone was throbbing. He spoke to
the face.

"Get out."

It was gone. But he did not know where. In the darkness
of the oaks he stood frowning. He was no stranger to things
like this: secret shadows and shapes, earth-things that the
land had bred and few men ever saw. Wirrun had seen and
spoken to some and was wary of them all; good or evil by
chance, most of them, and knowing neither good nor evil.
But none had burnt him with sudden angry hate as this one
had. It made him careful.

He kept his hand still on the netted bag and strode into
the light of the late afternoon. Leaving his firewood where
it lay he went quickly back to the creek, looking with narrowed eyes as he went for the patch of blue that meant Murra,
safely there. He came on half running and when he reached
her began at once to stow things back in his pack. Murra stood
staring, the cleaned fish in her hands.

"Wrap it in leaves and give it here," he told her. "We're
moving out."

"But the sun has gone! Even from above it is going!"

"I know that—it'll be dark by the time we get up there. So
we better move. We're not stopping here."

She saw that there was a reason and ran to pull leaves
while he filled a waterbag at the creek.

The light drained away as they climbed out of the gorge.
A thousand miles to the west the land still lay in sunlight
but east along the coast it was dark already. That long coast
lay under stars with a pale ruffle of sea along its edge; wearing scattered brooches of lights where the towns were clus-
tered, and here and there pricked with a light from an Inlander's home. But most of it, lying under the edge of
night, was in darkness.

It was a darkness that lived and moved, full of the small,
separate lives that hide by day: the flutter of moths, the

bumbling of beetles and the soft beat of feathers. Possums scolded in trees, bandicoots explored gardens for snails, wallabies swung silently over fences to investigate crops. And among them were inhabitants even older and more secret, the earth-things and powers and spirits of the land. And these were restless and angry, and some of them afraid.

Near the Cape one of them, an Anurra bouncing in pursuit of frogs, found in its way a thing that was a stranger—a thing with red eyes and no body. It bounced off again in sulky rage. Farther south in a scrap of rain forest a group of small man-shaped Dinderi stood gazing at red eyes among the ferns. Though the thing was a stranger to them too they did not order it off but grunted gravely to each other and went away and left it. A long way to the south a Dulugar, spindle-legged and hairy, found its mountain path blocked by a strange red-eyed face and flew off muttering among trees. Soon the eastern night was filled with angry mutters and whispers. Even old enemies whispered together like friends.

"Not of us," they whispered, and, "A dog-like thing, out of its place." And again, "Not our kind. A Man is needed." And as nights went by the whispers passed along the coast and grew.

"Where is the Hero, the Fighter of Ice, the Man with the power?" they whispered. "Where is the Hero?"

3

Wirrun and Murra had spent over a week in a gully, no more than a crease in the tangle of water-carved ridges that led to the coast. It was not a very good gully. Its trickle of creek fed only one small pool, and fish and yams were scarce. They stayed because Wirrun had come upon an Inlander who, like most, needed more help than he could afford. This one, caught in a late-summer accident of fire, was willing to pay a shabby passing stranger for a few days' fencing while he himself mustered several hundred head of straying stock; and as their way east brought Wirrun and Murra nearer to the countries of the Happy Folk Wirrun felt a need of money and accepted the job.

Murra did not approve. On several days she followed him from their camp to his work, within easy sight of the Inlander's white timber house; and since she wore only the old blue shirt that a white man would find outlandish, and since she put on her sharply teasing face and would not go away, Wirrun worked with one uneasy eye on the house and the other watching for a stranger.

Her reasons for disapproving were several. "I need not trouble to stay with you," she told him coldly, watching him work, "for you leave me alone to go and play with your crazy job and the money. You do not want me."

He could only mutter, "You know better than that," and hammer all the harder at a steel post. He could never appeal to her, or try to hold her with reminders of how alone he had been before she came or the sense of home she had

brought. He could not remind her of his one friend lost—
and nameless now, since the dead must not be named—
drowned in a dark cavern far away so that Wirrun might live,
and Murra too. But perhaps his face reminded her for she
said no more on that line.

"Why do you need this crazy money?" she demanded instead. "You have told me it is finished, all this of the towns
and jobs and money; and already you seek it again. Do we
not camp where we please and take what we need? Why do
you look for money?"

"To buy you a dress," he said patiently, having explained
before when he first accepted the job. "That old shirt won't
hold together another month—or my shorts either, come to
that. One of these days we'll run into someone and sooner
than you think. I won't have 'em looking at you like something the cat dragged in."

She was indignant. "But for this I wear the shirt, that they
will not stare—you have told me! Am I not beautiful in the
shirt?" She dragged it off and stood in her own lovely shape.

"Put it on," ordered Wirrun sternly, his eyes on the house.
"I don't try and teach you about catching fish. Don't you try
and teach me about gear."

After a moment she pulled the shirt on again. "I wear it
only to please you," she said grandly, "and not for any need.
I am beautiful without your dress, a thing I cannot help, for
I am Yunggamurra. To be Yunggamurra is to be beautiful
when the cat drags you."

"To be Yunggamurra is to be tickled if you don't watch
out. Any rate, you're not. You're my wife now." But he knew
that in spite of his Clever Business, the magic with the smoke,
she would always be partly Yunggamurra.

He had found her in a cavern deep under the ground, a
Yunggamurra from some far-off river, a silver water-spirit
with a song to trap men; carried off in a storm and lost and
caught in the dark, no longer knowing where her country
lay. He had brought her out, but since neither of them knew

her home he could not take her there; and so he had smoked the magic out of her and made her a golden-brown girl and his wife. For Wirrun she had put new gold into the sun.

He named her Murra. He dressed her in the old blue shirt and she was lovelier than any human girl, lovely as rain in sunlight or weed in water. He taught her tenderness and she taught him laughter. He showed her the foods of her new dry world, and how to set snares and roast yams in a fire, but not the skills of hunting and finding; she drew those skills out of the land itself and had done so for an age before the coming of white men.

Even when she told him of the wicked Yunggamurra game, and that one day her sisters would come to take her away from him, he refused to be afraid.

"If you want to stop with me you'll stop," he said.

She looked at him with eyes as old as rivers or moonlight. "You followed my singing only because you would? It is easy to be called and not to come?"

He laughed, for now he was happy and had forgotten that burning torment. He had only to watch her in the old blue shirt running like sunlight over unbending grass, or sitting alert by the fire she did not yet trust while the cloud of dark hair moved of itself on her shoulders as if it still floated, and he tingled with a delight he could never speak. He said, "I'd be following yet if I hadn't caught up. I was lonely for you, water-girl—needed you all my life."

Once, he could tell her; not again. After that he could only watch and hope that the water-girl was happy. He had watched her playing in creek after creek, all the water-games she had invented to replace the games of her sisters. He had seen the old blue shirt flowering high in the branches of gums, turning him cold with fear while she invented tree-top games. Wherever they stayed, even for a day, it was the same: undefeated, enduring, Murra filled that place with laughter and made it her own—and left it with pretended indifference, looking back. No place, it seemed, would hold to her; but she had seemed happy in all of them till now.

"What's wrong, any rate?" he asked her. "Don't you like it here?"

She lifted her head as if she were listening, and the dark hair moved on her shoulders. "I feel the west behind me," she said, and shivered.

Wirrun was glad when the fencing was done and he came back to camp for the last time with the money in good ready cash in his pocket.

Murra was there already, catching yabbies. He showed her the money. She poked it with a cautious finger and gave him a sly upward look. He snatched the money away and put it back safe in his pocket in case it should end at the bottom of the pool. She laughed and turned back to the water, dipping a rabbit's tail gently in to coax another clawed yabby within reach of her fingers.

Wirrun went to rake out the ashes of their old fire and lay sticks and leaves for a new one. He brought wood from a heap he had built in the shelter of stringybarks, lit his fire and set stones to hold a billy for boiling the yabbies. By then it was dusk; he could just see Murra at the top of the pool where the water trickled in, playing one of her water-games. It was an old one that she had played in many pools: sitting in the space between stones through which the water flowed, damming it with her body while it built up behind her, letting herself go with it at last to wash down into the pool. He smiled a little and went to bring more wood, taking his torch for it would be darker still among the stringybarks.

They were young trees. Leaves brushed his face as the twigs parted to let him through. He flashed his torch at the woodheap, reminding himself to add batteries to his shopping-list for the day when he reached a town. The torch-beam wavered as he went forward, making shadows jump aside and leaves flash silver-green. He stopped suddenly and turned the beam to one side: there was surely a shadow that had not jumped aside. His hand closing on the net bag at his belt, Wirrun spoke to it.

"What are you?"

The shadow moved. It was a shadowy woman-shape with horned shoulders, a shape he knew even before it spoke. It was the earth-thing Yaho, from his old country in the south. It said, "I come from Ko-in, Hero."

Wirrun relaxed. Ko-in: the ancient spirit-hero, the tall wise shadow that had sent him to find the netted bag he wore with its secret stone of power; Ko-in who had named Wirrun hero. Ko-in had sent this messenger before.

"What does Ko-in say?" he asked the shadow.

"That he must speak with you. He calls you to his country, to light your fire in the old place. Ko-in says that if you come fast you may come ahead of trouble."

"Hum," said Wirrun. "Maybe I don't travel as quick as trouble. It's a long way. Ko-in, now: he travels very fast. If he's in a hurry can't he come and talk here?"

"A time of trouble is no time for a Great One to be out of his place. But all countries are yours and your place is where you are."

"Hum," said Wirrun again, but he could not refuse a summons from Ko-in. "Tell him there's a lot of strange road between me and him and the winds don't always blow right but I'll come as soon as I can. It won't be under a week or two."

"The Great One knows you travel at a man's pace but he bids you travel safe. He sends a warning."

"That's something. Let's have it, then."

"Keep your hand near the stone of power—"

"No worries. Tell Ko-in I'm not a kid."

He thought the shadow gave a small malicious smile as it went on: "—and know always that you have mated with magic. It will swallow you or you will grow."

Wirrun frowned. "That's my worry. Get yourself back to Ko-in and say I'm on my way."

The shadow melted into others. Wirrun gathered his

armload of wood and went back to the fire. He thought of the maps in his pack: east to the coast and south, it must be a thousand miles—most of them fenced from now on, and under the watchful eye of some Inlander. And what sort of trouble worried Ko-in that he couldn't handle for himself?

Mated with magic . . . that angered him. He wasn't the first. Sure, he didn't know the Yunggamurra or their country, but tales were told at campfires across the land of men who caught and married water-spirits. But *keep your hand near the stone:* Ko-in must know his hand was never far from it. There must be some special danger that Ko-in dreaded; something that did not keep to its own country as men and spirits should do but lay all along Wirrun's road. He thought for a moment of menacing red eyes that glowed in a face without a body, but he put the memory aside. His own quick angry hate had made him believe those eyes meant something else. He had not told Murra about them.

He did not tell her, either, while the yabbies boiled and she crouched near watching them turn red; or later while she and Wirrun ate and talked about this summons from Ko-in; or while they packed food and gear to be ready for the journey. He did not tell her about the face until much later. Yet tonight, making ready to travel on east as she had wished, her eyes seemed full of shadows and questions.

They left the gully next morning when the heights were lit with early sun. They climbed up to those heights, for even white men, if they had to travel this country at all, knew better than to travel by the waterways and rugged slopes. Wirrun drew down his brows against the sun and tried to peer east, for he wanted to reach the coast by a route as direct as gorges and gullies would allow and from there to travel south by faster roads.

Even so early the wind pushed at them fitfully, for that was a windy country, standing as it did above the coastal plains and reaching away to the west. As the sun rose higher and Wirrun could see east more easily, the wind rose too, and pushed more roughly and pointed another way with trees. And Wirrun began to look sharply and feel the wind, for the way it pointed was nearer to his true one: south-east. At last he stopped.

"This is a right wind, girl," he said. "Will we take it?"

She looked frightened for a minute and then excited. She had heard about winds from Wirrun, and had played in tree-tops that were bending as these did. She waited, watching him.

He opened the net bag that held the power and unrolled a length of the grey cord it was wound in. The end of the cord he tied to her wrist for safety, in case she should lose hold of his hand. Then he settled the pack on his shoulders more firmly and took a good grip of the net bag in one hand and Murra's own hand in his other and swung her round.

"Come on, now—turn round and run into it."

They ran hand in hand into the wind.

It took them and tumbled them and flung them above trees. They clung together breathless and laughing. The wind tossed them higher and spun them around, they rose into it like swimmers lifted on some enormous wave and hand in hand were carried away: south-east in sunlight.

TWO

The Hero and the Water-Girl

I

Murra rode the wind with an instant skill that made Wirrun feel heavily earth-bound—her delight came to him through her fingers, throbbing like a pulse. In a moment she slipped her hand out of his and rode free on the lengthening cord of fur. Lifting like a feather she cried out: "I can see it—I can see it! The wind is a river!"

He too could sometimes see the stream and eddy of the wind as he had seen heat rising from a roof. Now he saw a Yunggamurra riding the stream: slipping in and out of currents, hanging like foam above depths, wrapped and unwrapped in her floating hair; and he saw with a pang that he, who lent her the power to ride it, could never fully share with her the river of the wind.

They crossed low over a ridge and she darted to the end of the cord, laughing like bubbles, to chase a startled magpie. She turned to wait for him, and he saw the laughter go out of her as she looked into the blue-hazed sky of the west.

He scolded her. "We're going ten times faster than we could down there. What are you scared of, any rate? Do you think your sisters'll come whizzing down out of the sky and grab you? They're water-spirits, aren't they? They'd be dried up into dust."

She looked at him gravely for a moment, then smiled. He reached for her hand and pulled her closer. "I wish you'd just forget about 'em. I told you before—if you want to stop with me you'll stop. People do what they want when they come right down to it."

She said nothing for a time but rode the wind beside him, looking down at the patterns of the land. When she spoke again it seemed not Murra, the teasing girl who had just chased a magpie, but something old and grave that spoke with warning.

She said, "Look below you, Hero. There is the land from which we are made, you and I, and does it not keep its own laws? Once it raised itself up and swallowed seas; they lie under it still. My kind remember them for we live long and remember much. It had proud rivers and tall forests then. See it now, this land, tired and old, worn down with sun and wind; for that is the law of lands. Am I more than the land? Must I not keep old laws? Look down, Hero."

He looked. The tired heights circled their secret valleys; stranded rivers vanished into hidden, guarded waters. The rough old rock was wearing into soil, the trees turned their grey leaves edge-on to the sun. He said soberly, "She don't give in, any rate; she creeps back another way."

Murra's eyes were as still and concealing as moonlight.

The day drew on. The country, grey-stubbled with forest, gave way to rolling grasslands with odd single peaks lifting out of them here and there. By late afternoon there were greener hills and sometimes, beyond them, a glimpse of the eastern sky low down, edged with a shimmer of sea. Wirrun had begun to watch for roads, for forest with water and a town near at hand. He could feel the wind beginning to fumble and had brought himself and Murra lower by loosening and tightening his grip on the stone of power.

They came down on a ridge with a road along its western side, a creek at its base and its spine clad in the rich dark green of rain forest. Wirrun had seen the roofs of a town under its southern tip: he could do his shopping early tomorrow while Murra waited safely in the forest.

They came tumbling into long grass near the road, Murra bubbling with laughter as she tried to stand. "I am too heavy!" she cried. "I have been too long in the wind's river and yet I saw no fish. Where were the fish?"

"Feathered fish," said Wirrun drawing her up. "I saw you go after a few." He took her quickly across the road, under a fence and into the forest.

They passed through its ragged edges of lantana and bracken and inkberry; beyond these the forest received them into stillness and a green water-light. Fern and fungus, moss-cushion and palm and downward-looping liana were posed as precisely as weed or sponge in a pool. Buttressed trunks stood close and soared high, beyond staghorn and crowsnest ferns clinging to upper branches, up and up to the green-lit surface of leaves. Murra walked between them wondering.

They went deeper in where a small plume of smoke would be lost before it cleared the forest canopy, and found a place with damp stones to build a fireplace and a springy bed of leaves to sleep on. There was no wood for a fire; all that had fallen was rotting with damp and green with moss. Wirrun left Murra to unpack what they needed for the night while he went back and forth the way they had come bringing wood from outside.

Murra curled up in a lap of great roots to feel the solemn height of the forest . . . and beyond it the strange eastern sea . . . and westward, reaching across the world, the old worn land over which they had come. It was one great quiet into which she sank, not hearing Wirrun come back and drop a load of wood in the leaves and go away. She let the quiet enfold her like water . . . and felt in it a trickle of something warm and needing . . . something small and simple and profound. Murra, the ancient hunter, smiled a little; she closed her eyes and went seeking, following that trickle of need.

A small thing, alive and old in the land. Driven by some warm dark need. A turtle—a snakeneck—working at a hole near the creek. Now she began to lay—her brooding satisfaction flowed into Murra too . . . When Murra opened her eyes Wirrun had brought another load of wood and was laying the fire.

"There will be turtle-eggs tomorrow," she told him.

"Good," said Wirrun to whom this sort of thing was no longer new. "I walk half a mile to get a bit of wood and you find turtle-eggs just sitting here."

She smiled and began to unpack, and then to cut up a rabbit they had brought.

They were both tired from the long day of sun and the pushing of wind at their backs. They built up their fire and put the rabbit on to stew, and while it cooked the dark came down in the forest while outside the sky was still streaked with red and gold. The dark brought curious rustlings, and small glinting lights like fireflies. Murra watched and listened sharply for a moment and then let her mind follow other sounds: the grunt of a possum, the screech and quarrel of fruit-bats in some fig. But Wirrun laid his hand on the power and spoke to the little lights.

"Come and talk."

They came slowly and unwillingly, little dark man-shapes that gathered at the edge of the light. It was their eyes that caught the fire and glinted red and yellow.

"What are you?" he asked them.

They answered in grunts with their eyes on the fire. "Dinderi, we." "Older than People."

He understood. They were claiming not only the age of all spirits but a precedence in the land. For a time that flowed back into dreaming, his People had lived in the land till it made them its own; and into their fears and dreams it had sent the earth-things. They and the People were related; they inhabited each other's lore and shaped and were shaped by it. But a few earth-things, like the tenuous Mimi of the north, were old beyond even the dreaming of the People—shaped, maybe, from the fears and dreams of long-forgotten men. This was the precedence that the little Dinderi claimed.

He offered them stew but they shook their heads though their eyes never left the fire. He made another guess.

"You want fire? Take some of ours, we got plenty."

But this too was the wrong guess. All the eyes darted fiercely at him and away, voices buzzed with anger.

"Ours, all ours!" "Plenty fire, we!" "You got ours!"

Wirrun was astonished. "*This* fire's yours?"

"All ours,": growled one of them again. "Older than People, we. Got fire. People came, got no fire. Stole it. Ours."

Wirrun considered. There were many tales of the coming of fire, but he was in the country of the Dinderi now and wanted no ill-will.

He said, "We thank you for fire. Take ours any time—it's yours."

They stirred, blinked at the fire now misting under ash, and in a little while drifted away.

"They are pleased," murmured Murra, having placed the direction of the fig tree. "I hear them whisper beyond the fire."

That troubled him. He sat staring into the dark for some time before he spoke. Then he said, "Don't you feel sad? Listening to 'em out there—and shut off? Don't you want to go back?"

To be a silver ripple on the water, he meant, a thing made of sunlight and rivers; to be one in the games, one voice in the singing; to live long and remember much.

She knew what he meant. "No," she said, "for then I had no name. There was nothing to name. There were only the Yunggamurra, all as one. But I am Murra, and she is the wife of Wirrun. And the fire is warm, and though you spoil the food with cooking yet it is sweet. I want to be here with you."

They sat in their separate silences, the shabby young hero and the water-girl in a blue cotton shirt, and each was suddenly alone. For he knew that with his gift of a name came other gifts that she must choose though she had no need of them: his gifts of cold and hunger and illness and age and death. And she, even while she chose them, knew that the choice was not hers to make; her choice was not allowed. So they sat apart and the dark whispered and listened.

In the morning they woke early and breakfasted on yams and tea. Then Wirrun left Murra alone again—for the last time, he told her—to find turtle-eggs and figs while he went to do his shopping. She watched with reserve while he went down the road with a long stride and a sack on his shoulder, for she did not trust this game of shopping. And he went like a child to a party, not only to end his worry about a blue-shirted beauty in the land of the Happy Folk but dreaming also of sausages and flour.

2

Wirrun followed the road down the ridge until he saw below the roofs of the town; and then he stopped. He had been away from them for so long that he had forgotten towns. It suddenly seemed that in a world where Murra lived these could not also be real. But there was the town, quite real, and he knew it well though he had never seen it before.

He went on down: to the hot black streets and hot white pavements that he knew. There it was, small but true to its kind—the shuttle of cars and people, the papers shuffling in the gutters, the shop windows brilliant with happiness carefully priced. It was a child's balloon, kept aloft by its own tensions, and he was a child going to the party. He found the supermarket easily since he knew it best of all and took his trolley and began his round of the shelves.

Flour, matches, salt, tea—and sausages; torch batteries, a comb; tough drill shorts, knitted cotton shirts, rubber sandals . . . he had reached the racks of cotton frocks and was suddenly timid. A girl should choose her own.

He chose two in shining cotton, one watery-blue and one golden-green, both hanging loose from shoulder-straps and each with a large square pocket that he thought might often hold yams or a dead rabbit. Then he remembered soap and a towel, and went back for them.

He had to pass a table of cheap, bright knick-knacks meant to be bought and given away, and he paused there to look and smile. He would have liked to bring Murra a gift—something extra—a moment of astonished delight that she could throw away later if she chose; but he thought that was more

than he could manage. He grinned at the idea of bringing
her a fancy tile, a china cat, a brass ash-tray, wooden salad-
servers, plaster book-ends, a red-laquered trinket-box . . .
Idly he opened the box. It was lined with mirrors. He
bought it.

He was out of the store in half an hour, striding more
slowly up the ridge with his sack heavy on his back and
some of his money still in his pocket: a margin of safety in
the countries of the Happy Folk. He had reached the rain
forest within two hours of leaving it, and the day was still
young.

Murra had dug yams as well as turtle-eggs, and cooked
them in the last of the fire. She had gathered figs and lillipillis
to eat along the way. She gazed in fascination at the packets
and plastic-coated packages that emerged from Wirrun's
sack, pushed an exploring finger into the sausages and chewed
one end of the comb.

He offered her the dresses a little doubtfully. "Next time
you can come and pick your own."

"Two!" she cried in bewilderment, and took them and
sniffed at their colours and stroked their glazed shine while
he explained why there were two and how the shoulder-straps
worked and showed her the pockets.

"You did not say there would be pockets!" she cried, having envied Wirrun his. She tore off the shirt and began to
pull the dresses on, one after the other. He left her to do
that while he changed his own ragged shorts and shirt for
new ones. By then she happened to be wearing the blue
dress, so he quickly folded the other and stowed it in his
pack with the old blue shirt. She looked at him sharply.

"You are new like rain. We are both very fine. Yet you
say they will not stare."

"They can stare all they like now we're fine," said Wirrun.
He reached into the sack for the package he had left till last
and handed her the red-lacquered box.

"What is this?" she asked, not taking it.

"It's for you. It's a present."

She took it carefully. "Fire," she murmured, feeling the colour with her fingers and running one of them along the line of the lid.

"Open it," he said, and showed her how.

She lifted the lid—dropped it quickly—lifted it again a little way, peeped in and closed it again. She whispered, "Water . . . water and fire . . ."

"And you," said Wirrun; but she knew the face in the box was hers for she had often seen it looking at her out of water. She stood opening the box, peeping quickly and closing it again as if the water might run out, while Wirrun managed to store everything in his bulging pack. He lifted the canvas water-bag to strap it in place, found it empty and muttered with annoyance. He had once been carried far on his way by a wind, and set down in a wilderness, leaving most of his supplies and water behind. It was not a mistake he wanted to make twice, even though they were already late in starting.

"I will take your crazy bag to the creek and fill it any rate," said Murra, perky with the excitement of her red box and her new pocket.

Wirrun grinned. "Good girl. Wait by the fence. I won't be long. Just gotta stretch these straps a bit and make the fire safe." He passed her the water-bag and she went off between tall trunks, the bag in one hand and the trinket box in the other, singing softly.

Wirrun fought with buckles and straps a little longer, emptied the billy over the fire and raked it out for safety, hoisted the pack and shrugged it into place between his shoulders, and himself set off through the forest. The bulky pack was not properly balanced; he eased and settled it as he went, stumbling a little. The stumble turned him aside into walking-stick palms; he pushed through, regaining his balance—saw the narrow blunt-nosed head come swinging at him from the palms—yelled and leapt and swung as he landed to balance the heavy pack. The snake, a Brown, poured its long body between stones and fern.

Wirrun stood still for a moment to slow his pulse and his breathing, thankful that the snake, having waited for a heavy footfall to reach it, had struck only once and gone. A man didn't expect a Brown to behave in either of those ways, and hampered by his pack he could easily have been in trouble. In the cool and damp of the forest, perhaps the snake had already felt winter coming and grown lazy. The moment was over: he took a deep breath and saw, with a jerk of his nerves, other shadows moving in the palms.

Three or four small Dinderi were crouched there. They looked with grave unblinking eyes from him to something half hidden in moss and dead leaves. Wirrun's hand closed on the power: he saw only the glow of red eyes but he knew what lay in the leaves.

"Get out," he barked for the second time.

The thing with no body looked at him for half a moment, knowing and menacing. Then it was gone.

"Cheeky like a dog," said the Dinderi.

"Why didn't you send it off, then?" Wirrun growled. He saw that the Dinderi rejected this thing and therefore the forest was not its place. "Are you scared of it?"

They shook their heads. "Older than People, we," they said.

He did not pause to wonder what they meant; he was full of an urgency he had felt before. The thing had gone, he did not know where, and Murra was waiting at the fence. He went after her. But as he went he thought swiftly of other fearful things he had seen—men of ice, a stone monster, the old and terrible Bunyip and others more strange; and he wondered why this thing of red eyes and no body should chill him more. For it seemed less than they; clumsy and unfinished, a drawing by a child, a no-thing; yet it chilled and angered him.

Murra was waiting by the fence, opening her red box a little wider than she had dared to do before and peeping a little longer. "See," she said, giving him a quick glimpse, "I have caught a tree."

He grinned in congratulation and because he was so glad to find her safe; but there was a question in his mind that had to be asked if he could ask it. He lowered his pack over the fence and climbed through. It was a question he wished he need not ask while she felt the west behind her.

She gave him the water-bag and he strapped it in place and lifted the pack again. "Didn't catch a Yunggamurra in the creek, then?" he asked, pretending to tease.

She closed the box and looked at him, gravely surprised; for her sisters, who would one day come to take her home, were not a matter for teasing.

"No," he said quickly, "all these rivers over here flow east. Any rate, they wouldn't come themselves. Too far for 'em, little silver things like that. They'd send a friend, some other thing."

She considered what he said or else she considered him, and after a moment answered quite directly. "Their laws are for the Yunggamurra and no other thing. Only they will come."

He would have to think about that—and turn her away from thinking if he could. He told her about the snake and that too she considered gravely.

And now at last they were free to travel the white men's roads in the eastern country: clothed like any other couple and with a little money in case they might need the white man's power. They set off down the ridge on their long journey to Ko-in's country.

3

The green plains and valleys of the east were edged by hills
and criss-crossed by roads. Little towns were strung like beads
on the roads, and cars scuttled between; the coast was lined
with holiday beaches. Wirrun and Murra avoided them all.

They kept among hills, using dusty country roads when
they could but letting the highways lead them from a distance. This was Inlander country: cars were fewer, towns
smaller and easy to avoid, houses could be passed at a distance. There was always a place to camp and food to be
gathered. Sometimes the hills stood close, looking down at
them with faces of stone or slopes of forest; sometimes they
were farther off, blue and shadowed with purple, shifting a
little stealthy and unseen. Sometimes the roads crawled over
their sides, and Wirrun and Murra looked down from
heights at green plains, east-flowing rivers, and the sea at
the hem of the sky.

They were already a long way south since the wind had
put them on their way, but still they had a long way to go.
Yet they travelled fast. There was something abroad that
hurried them on, melting the miles in front. Once they
were lifted by another wind and carried far south in a
day; often they stumbled on easier, straighter roads than
those on Wirrun's map and were led by shortened routes;
sometimes a car with a dark-skinned driver stopped to give
them a lift. Murra as well as Wirrun noticed how they were
hurried on and sometimes she was silent.

"What shall I do," she asked him, when a carload of the
People had set them down after a drive of a hundred miles

in two hours, "if this Grandfather Ko-in calls you to travel west? For trouble may be anywhere but all the land is west." He frowned. "Not all—not Ko-in's, or the south countries. No use wondering any rate. We'll have to wait and see." But he did wonder.

The eyes of these People who drove them always caught and returned to the net bag on Wirrun's belt; they looked away in sudden awe and stole glances from under their brows at the lovely girl with floating hair who carried a red box. Sometimes they told an old tale of their country, or of strange things they had seen, and waited; and Wirrun, understanding, would tell them in return about tailed women in a cave or the icy green-eyed Ninya from under the desert. And as word spread among the People the way to the south grew easier: a driver watched by the road to take them on, or a woman waited in the evening to bring them to a meal in a cottage.

There were nights in shanties on the edges of towns when old men talked and young men listened; and Wirrun, who was hero but young like the others, was strengthened too. There were nights when Murra sang sharp and sweet like a bird of the green eastern countries: of rain sinking and roots spreading and of tall proud trees; and the People listened and were silent. And here and there along the coast there were nights when Wirrun heard at last the name of Jimmy Ginger.

The story was told again and again of Jimmy, that sober and capable fisherman who on a clear, still day had tangled himself in his own prawn-net and drowned; and whenever it was told the men sat waiting, their eyes on Wirrun. He could only shake his head—but his skin began to prickle at the name of Jimmy Ginger, and more than once he thought of the snake in the forest and the red eyes in the leaves, and of Ko-in's warning. He never mentioned the unfinished thing, the no-face; partly because he knew nothing of it yet and partly because he still could not understand his own dark anger. He had only a feeling that this thing was somehow apart from others—there was some more knowing evil in the eyes, a less innocent evil.

Those were good days and nights for Wirrun, at home among the People; days and nights of a kind that he would never know again. Yet as the journey seized them and hurried them on, the travellers clung more to their days and nights alone. For it seemed that days and nights, like hills and rivers, would not hold to them any more. All the wide land was focused on the point of here, the immensity of time was sharpened to the point of now. The hero and the water-girl were glad of days when they walked alone on some white man's land through brown seeding grass, and of nights when they cooked what they had caught or gathered at their own fire, and afterwards Murra begged to be told again how Wirrun became the hero Ice-Fighter; for that was a name she heard often, both among the People and whispered beyond the fire.

He always hunched a shoulder when she asked him, for she had heard the tale often enough and he was afraid she was secretly laughing at him. But Murra would coax and tease, tug at his hair, stroke him gently where the gills would be if only he were a fish, struggle away from his defensive tickling, till at last he gave in and told her again.

He told her how the land, threatened by ice, had called on him to leave his job and fight against the Ninya; how Ko-in had led him to find the ancient power of his People where a dying man had hidden it long ago; about a great stone monster worn away by time, and spirits and earth-things of countries far from hers. And she listened soberly, for these were things she understood.

"Truly you are a hero out of your time," she said once.

"Not me. It's the power. I'm only the man that holds it."

She smiled a little. "And what man held it first? Who wound it in fur and hung it in a bag?"

"Eh?" said Wirrun. "That was a long time back. There's no way a man could know."

"But others could, of my kind. They know this power and

obey it in all their countries. Yet they name it only from you: Ice-Fighter's stone."

Later, when they lay in a blanket under the stars, Murra would watch the sky unsleeping and listen to the whispers beyond the fire; and she would know that she too was known. The silver water-spirit from a country far away, turned to gold and browned by the sun, dressed in a cheap cotton frock from a chain store: these others knew her.

So the journey hurried them on, but when they could they clung to now and watched the blue hills turn. When they found a river quiet between the hills they stopped to swim or fish and keep the river there. They lingered in a valley to snare rabbits and preserve the valley. They crossed the border of two states among trees so grand and graceful that Wirrun was silent and Murra remembered when forests and rivers were new. South again they went, between tall hills crowned with rock that turned the wind aside, and there they found a river that travelled with them. They came on it again and again, its main stream or its backwaters, and knew it by its feel.

"It's the big one," said Wirrun. Here in the hills it looked as small as another but Murra, knowing rivers, eyed it with respect.

It met them in every valley, and when a ridge of hills took them eastward over the plains it opened broad full arms and enfolded the hills. Towns and canefields clung to it, it grew rank with the smell of dairies and sharp with the smell of the sea; but always there were lonely banks and swamps where the swamp-lights played, and the river led them through. They stood at last on a ridge with the river behind, and in front a sheet of water, miles across, that the river filled in passing. This wide water stretched away to the west where far hills melted into sky. White cloud fanned over it, stilled yet full of force. And Murra, with the dark hair moving on her shoulders, said, "If you must go west I will wait for you here."

"Have sense!" snorted Wirrun, for half the world lay

open to the west that she feared, and the clouds hurtled out of it like a great white explosion. "How could I go off and leave you here?"

She followed his eyes. "We will stay a little any rate and catch new fish, for this is sea-tainted water and sea-things live in it." She turned to him and smiled. "My sisters would never come into this water, it would burn them. It is not water for Yunggamurra but only for Murra."

They went down the ridge through stringybark and iron-bark trees and found a path through a fringe of swamp. They left their things under the oaks that cried thinly in the wind. The water was shallow and warm, not fresh and not salt. They went out through deep soft mud, laughing as it dragged at their feet, past beds of weed into deeper places. A flock of coot rose with a noise like the crackle of fire, pelican looked on solemnly, and from over the water came a gentle argument of swans.

They found mud-crabs and chased eels and swam in the deeper channels with young sharks and other things of the sea. They caught mullet and bream and carried them back through the shallows. Murra gave a teasing call and vanished into a bed of weeds and was lost for ten minutes. He knew she was there, and that now she was nearly human and had to breathe, but he could not find her till she appeared again with a tangle of weed in her hair.

They took their catch to the shore and laughed again at the mud and tried to wash it off. The river-oaks trampled the risen tide under their roots. Wirrun and Murra went back through the swamp and up a small gully among lilli-pillis, and made a fire by its trickle of water to cook their fish. The afternoon grew close and warm, and after they had eaten they slept.

When Wirrun woke it seemed dark under the trees. He looked for a patch of sky: it was purple and green like an old bruise, and while he was still gathering his wits the thunder growled. He began to throw things into his pack, casting about in his mind for shelter. The trees stirred anxiously and were still again. The river-oaks cried and were silent.

"Murra!" he cried. "Wake up, girl! There's a storm brewing."

A fierce blue flash ripped the dark. Murra was up, seizing her red box and a packet of salt. She was suddenly still: her eyes aged and she stood holding the box and the salt. She dropped them and went running through the scrub. Wirrun shoved his pack under a log and went after her.

"Murra! Where are you going?"

She stood at the edge of the scrub looking down over the water, and her eyes were wide with fear.

"Murra, girl!"

She shrieked: "No—not yet—one small summer—" Then she was running again.

He ran too. The trees cried out and a great fist of wind shoved him back. A whiteness of rain came roaring over the water. Lightning slashed, thunder cracked, and he ran on. He could see Murra running through the swamp—the wind threw her green-gold dress back at him. He lost her in the shrieking oaks but he knew where she was: in the sea-tainted water, fighting through mud, making for the weeds.

He followed through the howling oaks into stinging rain and hammers of wind and on into churning water where the mud gripped his feet and he stopped. Which weeds? There was no sign. He too was afraid, for above the shout and shriek of the storm he began to hear another sound and he knew it.

There was a high, sweet singing in the heart of the storm He knew those voices, sharply sweet like wild honey. They had come for her, the Yunggamurra sisters.

He plunged deeper into mud gripping the power and shouting. "Get off—get off!" But the stone did not throb or the voices falter: they were too far and high, the power did not reach them. All the other voices of the storm were hushed, it seemed, and gave way to the singing that pleaded and charmed, the notes that came falling like leaves through the rain. He could not hear the words for they were not sung to him, but their sweet and sorrowful pleading burnt him. Yet the water-girl did not come.

He thought he could see wind-tangled hair flying in the clouds, and lightning-gleams on silver twining limbs. "Get off!" he called uselessly again, for the voices tore even him. But the water-girl did not come.

Then the singing wavered and broke, and the voices rose in a sound as wild and haunting as a man could hear. A wild lone howling filled the sky and wavered and mourned; it was as if a pack of dingoes ran through the storm. Wirrun was stilled and shivered. Then he saw.

Through the screen of the rain came a tall column of water, twisting, circling, its head leaning into cloud. It was brown with sucked-up mud and weed, fish flew in it and fell. Silver long-nailed hands reached down from the clouds and the Yunggamurra mourned and howled. He saw one small brown hand break up from the water, and the column reached for it and she was drawn up wrapped in the darkness of her hair and taken into the storm. The column swayed and shattered.

Wirrun came to himself waist-deep in water with his feet trapped in mud and knew it was useless to shout any more; she was far away. They had not come into the sea-tainted water; they had called her out to the deep channels with the young sharks. They had drawn her out of hiding— she had made her choice between now and forever.

In the heart of the storm she clung to her sisters for they were clever and cunning. Though pleading could not touch them they knew it would touch her: they had begged her— not to come home but only, for the sake of memory, to come nearer. Rolling in the wild wet turmoil of the storm she knew she had been right in the beginning. There was no choice; there had never been a choice.

THREE

The Death in the West

I

He had known all along, from the very first day; even when he refused to hear her warnings, he had known he could not keep her. A thing grown out of dreams and fears and time—out of water and sun and starlight—could not be tied to a wrinkled old age and death. Yunggamurra: that was the cruel and beautiful, vanishing thing that a man could not have. He knew it, yet he could not believe she was gone. Not yet, not really gone. Not forever.

She would escape from her sisters and come back. He sat on the ridge above the wide water and waited.

He watched all through the first night, flashing his torch from time to time so that she could find him. At dawn he told himself it was still too soon; she could not have come straight back, they would only have followed her. He ate cold baked yams and dozed a little in the shade—and woke with a start fearing she had come while he slept. When he had called and walked about in the open and found she was not there he thought of cooking a meal to have ready when she came. He took a possum from a hollow limb where he heard it scratching, and found dry firewood in the storm-wet scrub and made a fire.

When night came again he watched for a long time keeping the fire alive. Towards dawn he suddenly began to swear, and tore the cold baked possum apart and ate some. On the second morning he knew she would not come. He went on sitting where he was.

He was bitterly angry, holding the anger over something dark and terrible underneath.

In the evening he finished the possum and sat with his head on his knees, now and then impatiently reaching for something to throw on the fire. He did not look up when the leaves rustled over his head or when a shape dropped lightly down beside him.

The shape stood watching him, tall and commanding, a man of the People. It carried a firestick in one hand and wore a pattern of white pipeclay. It waited in silence for a moment and then spoke deeply.

"Greetings, Hero."

Wirrun looked up. "Ko-in," he muttered, and lowered his head again.

"Speak with me," the shape commanded.

Wirrun lifted his head for another moment and dropped it again. "Hi," he said.

The shape seemed to grow taller.

"Is it for this I leave my country in a time of trouble? Was it for this I hung that bag at your belt and called you hero? That you should sit here an empty mussel-shell, a nothing on a hill? Call back your manhood, Hero."

Wirrun's lips twisted into a kind of smile. "Yeah? And do what with it?"

Ko-in's eyes flashed. "The man who asks that is indeed an empty mussel-shell. I have called on you for help: is that nothing? Your friend lies nameless in the First Dark, a hero of your making unknown in his own country. Is that nothing?"

Wirrun stared sulkily at the fire. There was no answer to the second charge. To the first he growled, "You don't need no help. You got your own kind to help, and all the power you want between you. You can fix your own troubles better than what I can."

Ko-in snorted. "So says the Ice-Fighter to the one who made him and gave him help in his troubles. I have warned you, Hero—those who mate with magic are swallowed or they grow; there is no way between. And I do not choose that a hero of my making shall walk through the land an empty skin." He moved around the fire till he stood above Wirrun and spoke sternly. "I lay on you my need and the need of your friend. I give you a day to recall yourself—and to think if it is a small thing that brings me out of my country against my will. And when the sun lies on the hills again I will come back." He rose rustling through the leaves and was gone.

Wirrun sat on for a time, obstinately rigid. Then he shrugged, reached into his pack for a blanket, rolled himself in it and slept.

In the morning he looked for food and found nothing ready. He refused to trap or fish and made tea instead. When that proved not enough he gave in with irritation and used flour and salt from his pack to make a very bad damper, cooked too slowly in a fire with too much flame. He ate some of that and for a time moved restlessly about in the scrub, but he would not leave it. Even through its screen of leaves he could see, if he were not careful, glimpses of sleek still water, blue-grey, with a far shoreline of slate-grey trees beyond.

Yet as the day went on the scrub smothered him. He could not leave it and neither, he saw angrily, could he stay in it. He found himself thinking often of Ko-in and of the friend who must not be named but who was named in his heart: his friend Ularra. They invaded his mind, now one, now the other, in snatches of memory and echoes of words. Defensively he turned to his pack and began to stow away the things he had used. And at once he knew that this was no idle passing of time: he was packing to travel. He could not any longer sit idle in this poisoned place.

He packed sometimes fiercely and sometimes in confusion. A comb and a blue cotton dress he bundled tight and thrust hard into a rotted log. A faded cotton shirt he stared at helplessly and at last left it on the ground. He was fastening the pockets on his pack when his eyes caught a splash of red in dead leaves on the other side of the fire: the lac-

quered box. He reached for it to smash it . . . or shove it
under a log . . . *see, I have caught a tree* . . . he thrust it
deep into the last pocket and pulled the strap tight.

Now he could get away . . . but it wasn't time. He lay
down and went to sleep again. When the setting sun struck
low over the water and under the leaves of the scrub to
light his face, he woke. By then he had come to some sort
of terms with his deep and bitter pain. He could not see a
life ahead but he could see a step.

A man had debts. He would pay what he owed his friend;
and before he set out he would hear what Ko-in had to say.

He made fresh tea, ate more damper, and sat keeping the
fire up and staring at it. Ko-in came silently down through
the trees and stood watching. He had been there for some
time before Wirrun saw him and called to him.

"All right, old friend. Sit down and talk. And make it
good—I got work of my own to do."

"You are more right than you know," said Ko-in coming
forward. He folded himself down cross-legged by the fire.
"I speak to you not for my own country but for all the countries of the land." He waited.

"Go on," said Wirrun, waiting too.

"You were called once by the land and once by the People. Now I bring you the call of earth-things and spirits."

"I don't think I follow that," said Wirrun at once but
politely. "The land—well, she calls who she likes and the
ice was everyone's business. Maybe I was a sort of bridge
between white men, People, earth-things, the lot. After that
the People: well, fair enough; I was their own and who else
would they call? But now it looks like you want me to handle
your kind of trouble, the sort your kind could handle better
than me if you wanted to. Why me? I don't follow that."

"How should you," said Ko-in tartly, "when the cord is
not yet in your hand? I might claim the right of a gift for a
gift—for my kind gave you help when you called. But I see
you are not yet strong enough to remember your friends for
their own sake; I must put the cord in your hands and close

your fingers on it. You must answer the call of the earth-things because their trouble is of your making, not theirs. It is a trouble of man's making, a man of the People; and now it wanders and disturbs my kind."

Wirrun lowered his brow till his eyes were shadowed and looked darkly at Ko-in. "I still don't follow. What sort of thing can a man make that can trouble your kind?"

"A thing of power to rule him," said Ko-in looking darkly back. "A thing to be seen or unseen as it will, to go where the wind goes, to live from age to age. A thing to call men's spirits from their graves and take to itself the telling of right from wrong. An evil thing that calls itself death."

Wirrun's dulled mind had had no time to grasp at this. He was staring stupidly. "An—earth-thing? Made by a man?"

"No," said Ko-in strongly, "for earth-spirits grow from the land and know only its laws—as heroes grow from man's best self and know only that. There are earth-things that steal a man's spirit from its grave—that prey on living men—that bring sickness and death and fear and fire and whirl-wind—that are evil and yet know nothing of evil. This thing knows. It knows from its maker."

"It must know madness too, then," said Wirrun harshly. "What man would make a thing like that to rule him?" But his skin prickled. *This thing knows:* had he not seen an un-finished thing with fiery eyes that knew evil?

Ko-in smiled grimly. "A foolish man indeed, with a sing-ing too strong for him that he got from one a little wiser. A man hungry for power, who made the thing to serve him. A man too foolish to know that such a power would never serve but must rule."

They were silent for a while. Wirrun stared at the fire, trying to come to grips with a story so different from all he knew of the People's lore. Ko-in watched him.

"And see," he said in a moment, "how this thing takes its evil from its maker. It takes the power over life that he longed for, for to look at it is death to a man. It takes the greatness he sought, for it makes itself a judge of dead spirits and a maker of Clever Men. And as he made it, it makes others of its own kind to serve it. They are many and make trouble in that country."

Wirrun grunted in angry doubt. "I never heard of a thing like that in all the land."

"That is not strange for its country is far in the west, and there, where it was made, it must be borne like other fears. It is an old shame now and the land is very wide; only my kind still whisper of it. But now this hungry thing comes east. We have seen it, and not we only. A man is dead."

"What man?—how?"

"A man to be trusted, and one of the People. Taken dead from the sea, tangled in his own net."

In the fire Wirrun saw days and evenings that could not come again, and a worried waiting look in many eyes. "Jimmy Ginger," he said, and Ko-in nodded.

"Nothing outside its own country will endure this thing," he said sternly, "and none will meddle with it. A dog-like thing, a man's work, fit only for a man to master. We call on you, Hero: a man of power, and one to whom all countries are his own. The work is yours."

Wirrun frowned. "I don't know this thing—for all I can see, it makes no sense. There must be Clever Men in its own country; call on them. You talk about a gift for a gift, I reckon you've weighed that up on the wrong side. Your kind have cost me dear, man. Right now I wouldn't care if I never laid eyes on 'em again."

"And did you think," said Ko-in, "that if the great Ice-Fighter grasped at fire his hand would not burn? You should know, Man, that anger is a dog: its own ears are quick but its snarling stops its master's ears. We do not ask a gift, or for help. We call on you for rightness and the law. This is a man's work. You are the Man, the one fit to do it."

"I got work of my own, for one thing. For another, there's no man fit to do it. If this thing's come from far west right over here, it must be all over the land. How can a man cover that? It can't be done."

"When you journeyed at the land's call it gave you help. When you answered the call of the People they gave help. Are they earless, empty things that call you now?"

"You said they wouldn't meddle."

"Nor will they. But where they ask they also help and their footprints are in the whirlwind. Ask for no knowing or searching or doing; even your power will gain you nothing. But ask for yourself what you need and say only who you are. Ask to journey and you will arrive." Ko-in stood up. "Come, now. You have seen this thing yourself and yet you are alive: you must know you are the Man. And one dark angry sorrow has not killed all your spirit. You have work for your friend; that too lies west. Begin your journey for your friend and follow your own spirit from there. It may lead you on, and into many countries." He looked searchingly at Wirrun. "Even into the country of the Yungga-murra."

2

Wirrun rose slowly as if anger forced him up. He glared at Ko-in. In a moment he said tightly, "What's that mean? If it's a carrot for a donkey the carrot's rotten. You think I'm a fool?"

"I do not know," said Ko-in. "I do not need to know; the need is yours. But I would not send one I love on such a journey in any kind of need. Tell me, then: what are you?"

"I thought you had it off pat. Ice-Fighter, aren't I? Clever Man. The one with the power. That's what you said."

"That much I know. Beneath these stars and above these rocks it is very little. Are you no more?"

Wirrun clenched his hands.."I'll tell you. I'm a man. Of the People. It's all I want. It was you put the name of hero on me."

"Oh Man!" cried Ko-in. "And is that all your greatness? An axe falls on it. You are cut short. I am Man, I am hero, I am black—with every name an axe-blow. You see this fire? I see it in your eyes: a little fire, made small. All your names are yourself in the eyes of others; yourself made small."

"Forget 'em then," growled Wirrun, bitter and confused. But Ko-in seemed to tower and spoke with passion.

"I am hero, Ice-Fighter, Clever Man—with every name the axe falls, you are cut short! Poor spirit! Under all these blows how can it find the strength you need? Will you not speak for it? Will you not say what the stars will stoop to hear and the rocks answer?"

Wirrun only glowered again. But Ko-in was an ancient hero, one who had awed many ages of People; he could compel. Wirrun growled, "I'm—" and stumbled into silence. He could find no other name.

"When the need comes," said Ko-in, quite calmly now, "you may remember it." He laid a hand like a bat's wing on Wirrun's shoulder. "I give you what strength and rest I can. Take what you will and say where you will go, for word has been passed and they wait."

Dazed and emptied as he had been before by Ko-in, Wirrun reached for his pack. He had made no decisions and knew almost nothing of what he was supposed to hunt but the moment had caught him. Looking at Ko-in he said, "Take me . . . to old Tom Hunter, wherever he is . . . somewhere near Mount Conner."

Before he had finished speaking he felt a panting breath on his neck. He swung quickly to see firelight on leaf-shaped yellow eyes—on great white teeth and a tongue lolling red near his shoulder—on the shaggy shape of a huge black dog.

"Jugi!" he whispered, for he had seen one before at a distance and it had been dreadful then.

The dog crouched. Wirrun hesitated, then climbed on to its back, twisting his hands in the deep, strong hair. Its dog-smell was suffocating and the hair and body felt real, yet when it moved he felt no play of bone or muscle. There was only a gathering of power under him and a strong smooth flowing of himself and the dog through scrub.

He crouched down to keep leaves and twigs from whipping at his face and saw no more of the fire among the lillipillis or the scrub or the wide water. The power beneath him surged and flowed with a speed that blurred the pale new stars. They passed through evening into sunset down wide inward-sloping plains, and in a cupped red country hung with blue hazes they caught up with the hot gold glare of late afternoon. That was as much as Wirrun saw until he felt that surging power lean back into itself, and saw with the blood pounding in his head that they had stopped among ironwood trees on yellow rocks. The Jugi stood; he tumbled and slid from its back; it shook itself, gathered for a spring, and was gone. Wirrun fell back among rocks and lay there.

As the heat of the land's centre released its grip and began to rise he saw that he knew this place among the ironwoods. The Jugi had brought him not to Mount Conner but to a gap in ranges of jagged rock that walled a town. It must be here that he would find Tom Hunter, that steady man who had brought both Wirrun and Ularra here on the People's business—but it was hard to camp here now, where he and Ularra had camped. And it was a hard thing he had come back to do for his friend; he sat and thought about it where they two had sat before, while the hills of the red country turned apricot and gold in the sunset.

In a water-clear twilight he took his billy and went out of the ironwoods, side-stepping down the rocks to a wide dry river-bed below; for he knew that at this time there would be a few of the People somewhere along the river. He had been shown how to draw water from this river. He crossed its bed, grassed over between patches of sand, till he found where the old iron lid lay. It lifted back from a hole—it could not be called a well—dug only deep enough to reach the river's hidden water. He lowered his billy, glancing along the farther river-bank and up towards the town. A dark-skinned group, perhaps a family, watched him from the shade of tall ghost-gums. Lower down the bank and quite near, two small boys inspected him secretly while they pretended to gather wood.

He held up the billy and called to them. "Want a drink?"

They came, trying to stand behind each other, taking a few sips each from the billy while from under their long dark lashes their eyes travelled over him. Wirrun nodded towards the family watching from the bank.

"Your old man up there?"

They nodded.

"You give him a message for Tom Hunter. Tell him the Ice-Fighter's come." They stared at him. "Go on, now."

He waved them off and they scampered away like young

rabbits. Wirrun refilled his billy and covered the water again.

He strode back across the river-bed, climbed the rocks to his camp and lit the small fierce fire of the dry country to make tea. He ate the rest of his scorched dry damper with it, watching the fire and thinking, gathering together the threads of the story he had to tell so that the men of Ularra's country might understand his greatness; for Ko-in had hurled him like a spear into this work and he had to relive things that had been laid away.

It was painful remembering, and it held him so that he did not hear the tread of boots over rock or see the arrival of Tom Hunter. He only looked up to find the old man standing looking down: steady and dignified as always in his frayed trousers with an old waistcoat over his checked shirt, his grey-stubbled face and intent dark eyes catching the light of the flame. He carried a torch in one hand and in the other a white-wrapped parcel which he held out to Wirrun.

"Few chops," he said, but he did not smile.

Wirrun took the parcel uncertainly. "I'm not here on your business. That's done. I come to tell about him. Him that went with me."

"He's dead," said Tom. "We heard."

Wirrun knew they would have heard something since the journey had been their affair. The young men moving over the thousand-mile-tracks—from settlement to mission, to station or fishing-boat and back down the long roads—would have passed the news along.

"There's more," he said. "No one knows it all, only me. Are there men from Conner here?" For men drifted over many miles of sand and spinifex and mulga into this town.

"Jump-up," said Tom, "and I dunno who else. Enough to pass the word." He stepped back into the dark and flashed his torch.

Wirrun put more wood on the fire. He was cold, colder than the sharp desert night and the sharp bright stars. This time he heard the boots on rock, a number of them.

The men came out of the dark into his camp led by Tom Hunter's torch. They stood around the fire, a circle of dark eyes and faces catching the light. None of them smiled. He remembered some of the faces but looked only for Jump-up: older than Tom, more grizzled, his face deeply creased. Wirrun nodded to him. "You'll find a rock to sit on."

They all found places on rocks round the fire and sat gravely waiting. Wirrun knew that perhaps only two or three were men from Ularra's country near Mount Conner; the others had come to hear and support. But they came not only for Jump up and Ularra. They were the men who had called on him to quieten troubled earth-things wandering far from their own countries and to send them home; they came also to hear of that. He sorted the threads of his story and spoke.

"There was this singing got me. Out east before I come here. I never knew what it was. Never thought it was mixed up in your business."

They listened and waited. He told them in plain bare words how he and Ularra had found a cave; and the trouble was in it, and the singing too.

"Only he—he got himself caught too. Not the singing, not then. A different thing. She turned him." The shaggy hair, the long claws, the pleading eyes of the beast that had been his friend Ularra.

He told how in this need he had made a turning of his own and made the beast into his friend again. "It worked. Only he couldn't trust it. The beast—was too much for him. He couldn't forget . . ."

They shifted, in fear or pity. He told how he had left his friend safe, he thought, while he went into the cave and deep underground to find the singing, cause of all their trouble.

"But he knew, see. He knew I was sung. He came after me." Wirrun hunched closer to the fire. Himself and Ularra quarrelling in the ancient First Dark—bitter words—and the silver water-spirit with moonlit eyes singing them on. "He got past me—" Ularra's face in the water, so strongly at peace. "He knew—he let her drown him. To save me and be rid of the beast." He laid his head on his knees. "He was a hero."

The men were very still. After a moment Jump-up spoke. "Where is he?"

Wirrun lifted his head. "I couldn't bring him out. I did what I could." He told them that too.

"We'll do the rest," said Jump-up, and Wirrun nodded and waited. If they asked for the end of the story and the fate of the water-spirit he would have to say the words, whether they were understood or not. If they did not ask they could hear the words from someone else in time or perhaps had heard them already. The eyes were still grave and withdrawn. At last Tom Hunter spoke.

"What had to be done, you did it; the both of you."

The men nodded. He saw that they understood, and saw for the first time what drew them together against him. It was not anger or blame but awe: they were afraid of him. Three days ago he would have seen it with a bewildered sense of loss. Now he saw it wearily. Memory had drained out of him in the telling, leaving only something heavy and solid, a stone inside him.

"Where you going from here, then?" Jump-up asked after a pause.

"Eh?" said Wirrun; for he had already taken his one step and had made no more decisions. He stirred restlessly. "You know anything about a fiery-eyed thing that calls itself death?"

They looked uneasy and shook their heads. If he had been only young Wirrun who rode the wind and sent the ice-men home they might have said more. But he was an older Wirrun who had turned his friend from a beast back to a man and had seen dark things. The young men had not spoken to him at all.

"Don't anyone see it," he grunted; for they were all good men. Sound men, to be trusted. Men like Jimmy Ginger.

They saw his restlessness and rose to go. "Thanks, then,"

said Jump-up and they nodded. Seeing them turn away and Tom Hunter flashing his torch Wirrun found a sudden need and turned quickly for his pack, fumbling with a pocket. He spoke softly to Tom.

"See you in the morning?" He held up a little cash. "Bring a couple of cans."

Tom hesitated only a second, took the money and nodded, and turned away with the men. Wirrun listened to their boots drawing away down the rocks.

He had still made no decision. He felt only weary, dissatisfied and uncertain; and that Tom Hunter was a man who had listened at campfires in many countries of the west.

3

In the chill of that night Wirrun crept into his sleeping-bag: the first time he had used it since he and Murra lay in one blanket under the stars. He slept heavily but not well, dreaming of a death with red knowing eyes and waking before dawn with death in his mind.

Hunger and illness and age and death . . . *Truly you are a hero* . . .

. . . And is that all your greatness? An axe falls on it . . .

The stone inside him began to swell. If he were not careful it would turn into pain. As soon as it was light enough he shook himself free of the sleeping-bag and went down to the river-bed for water.

There were hours to be passed before Tom Hunter might come. He lit his fire, washed and shaved, changed to fresher clothes—making himself, if he had known it, a less awesome figure than he had been last night. He cooked and ate some of the chops Tom had brought. After that he sat avoiding memory, exploring his own dissatisfaction with the story Ko-in had told and what he had seen of the red-eyed thing; watching through the ironwoods the land gathering heat, the roofs of the town beginning to shimmer, the hills putting on their fragile, vivid blues.

At last he saw Tom coming down the river. He waited for the sound of the boots on rock and went to the edge of the shade. Tom carried a small sack that clinked as he walked. They nodded to each other and moved back to sit in the shade.

Wirrun said, "Thanks, mate. It's better here than showing up in town." Tom nodded again, reaching into his sack.

The beer in the dewy cans was still cool. Wirrun sipped it slowly; Tom drank and waited. After a minute Wirrun said, "You ever heard of a thing that calls itself death? Anywhere?"

It was easier to talk in daylight over a beer. Tom shook his head. "Spirit-chasers," he offered. "At graves. After dead men. There's plenty of them."

"I know them. You do the right things and you beat 'em. That's like—all the rest. I'm told this thing's different, you can't beat it. I never heard of anything like that." He sipped.

"There's one like that up north, round Katherine," said Tom. "They reckon a Clever Man made it a long time back and now it's got 'em."

Wirrun turned to him. "That's the one. Do they reckon"— he slowly turned the can in his hand, carefully approaching his own restless discontent with this tale of Ko-in's—"that it gets the lot of 'em in the end, then?"

Tom nodded and drank, wiping his chin afterwards. "Gets the lot and says which ones can go home. There's some gotta be cleaned up first with fire."

That was it: the incredible thing, the thing that fitted no lore of the People that Wirrun knew. He shook his head. "I know it's bad, I've seen it." Tom looked sideways at him and away. "But I never heard of anything like it."

"Worse because they made it theirselves," Tom suggested. "That's what we say." But Wirrun only nodded moodily so he emptied his can and opened another. They both brooded in silence. At last Tom thought of something. "I heard they got a thing out west, right down near them Stirling Ranges. I met a man once."

Wirrun raised frowning eyes. "Yeah?"

"He said they had something. I dunno much. A thing that gets after a man's spirit only there's one it wouldn't take. She was too bad for it. Would that be the same?"

"What's it called?"

Tom struggled. "I remember the woman best . . . Balyet, that's her. Young girl, pretty as a bird, caught lots of men. Two of 'em, blood-brothers, fought over her and killed each other. Worst thing that can happen over there, blood-brothers doing that. They wouldn't have this Balyet after that; wouldn't kill her and send her home. This—white thing— Noatch, that's it—it wouldn't have her either. Too bad for it. She's there yet. Calls little 'uns and young girls; puts her arms round 'em if she can get 'em, and they die real quiet." He glanced sideways at Wirrun. "Would this Noatch be any good? Too far, I reckon."

Wirrun gave a tight smile. "Not for me. They're taking me wherever I want. Do it under an hour."

"Ah," said Tom uncomfortably, but Wirrun didn't notice. He was thinking.

"This Noatch: what do they do for it? Can you remember if he said?"

Tom thought obligingly. "Fire," he said at last. "It's a cold thing, this. Goes to fire. Wants to get warm, or it's curious. You make a big fire, take it away from the little grave- fire. It'll go to the big one and the dead man gets away. No warmth, see."

"There you are, then," said Wirrun. "There's rules for it. Might take a look at it all the same." For he could not sit on among the ironwoods any more than he could have stayed in the eastern scrub, and he had not yet uncovered all his uneasiness about this northern death. He added, "I knew a man'd be able to count on you. Thanks, mate."

"Don't know if it's right," said Tom. "Don't you want this other can?"

"You have it. One'll do me, I'm not used to it."

"I'll go, then," said Tom getting to his feet, for he did not want to see Wirrun leave.

"No hurry—stay and finish the beer. I got all the time there is."

Tom stood looking down, and Wirrun could not see

whether his eyes held fear or pity. "You've gone too far ahead of us, boy. You got a bad job this time. We'll make a singing for you."

"You do," said Wirrun full of uncaring weariness. "That's what I need." He watched old Tom go out of the hot shade into the beating sun; watched to see him cross the river-bed and climb slowly up the farther bank. Then he saw to the remains of his fire and fastened his pack and hoisted it on.

As he did so he chose the words that would take him on the next journey. He did not want to face this white thing that might be a death; he wanted to observe it unseen, at least for a time. Somewhere near it, that was what he wanted. Gazing through trees at the river he said, "Take me to this Balyet."

The ground stirred: a small secret movement that rattled no stones. The river-bed was blotted out by a darkness. Something lay in it, something large and dark and coarsely textured with a fluid shape that might have been poured molten. Toes?—a foot? Wirrun's blood was singing and he clutched the power in reaction and the trees swayed and cracked as a great dark hand came down through them and closed over him. He was swept up above the broken trees into hot sunlight.

From the chest down he was gripped and enclosed in enormous fingers. He was swung above the river-bed and stared into teeth like white rocks. They opened and snapped, and through them came a laugh like a roaring wind. By staring up Wirrun could see the rest of the coarse-grained face. The Pungalunga shook its head, still laughing. Its body was an indistinct darkness going down into the river.

"Ice-Fighter!" it roared. "No fire-eyes round here, Man. Balyet, eh?" It held him firm and shaded against what must be its chest and took a step up on to the range. It paused there, and Wirrun looked down at fangs of rock with treetops between. Then the rushing journey began.

Swing and pause, swing and pause, half a mile at a swing with the wind drawing the air out of Wirrun's lungs till he

could scarcely breathe. He saw and felt only the pitted-
rubber skin of the Pungalunga, heard only the wind and
once or twice a deep shaking grunt. Swing and pause, swing
and pause . . . he was half hypnotised.

When the rhythm broke and slowed he was startled and
stiffened. The Pungalunga came to a stand, grunted again
and lowered its hands a little letting in the dazzle of light
and the stroke of heat.

"Coming, Ice-Fighter," it boomed. "Soon here."

He gathered himself together and looked, and first he saw
that the day was younger. Then he saw the miles of sand-
plain, red misted over with the grey of mallee scrub, that
reached away to a blur with the white dazzle of a salt-pan to
the north. Moving fast towards him against the hazy distance
a tall finger of red sand curled and beckoned: a willy-willy.
The Pungalunga stood like a tower on a low granite ridge
and waited.

When the whine and rustle of the willy-willy sounded
near, it said, "Jannoks here. Hands over face, Hero."

Wirrun's hands were already there for he knew what
that whirling column of wind and sand could do. The
Pungalunga swung him forward; there was a confused moment when wind smote, sand stung, bony hands plucked and
grabbed; then he was moving fast within a stillness, enclosed
in the rustle and scream of the willy-willy. He lowered his
hands and looked.

The funnel of the wind, dimmed by flying sand, was darkened by a funnel of dark bodies that swung and circled in
it. Those nearest held him firmly between them: they were
shapes like very old men, grey-haired and emu-footed. Now
and then they peered at him with bright curious eyes but
said nothing. Now and then, from high or low in the column
or near at hand, they screamed with the screaming wind. He
could not speak to them for the noise and speed and whirling, but for safety he shouted into the nearest ear: "Balyet!"

The Jannok nodded. "That rubbish!" it screamed, and
spat.

After a time the noise grew less and the light stronger. Between grey heads and brown shoulders he glimpsed sunlight and whirling leaves. The column wavered and shifted in shape and soon the old emu-footed men fanned wide on the wind, clustering about Wirrun in their centre. He saw that they blew over woods of mallee towards high rocky crags where the mist curled; and while he, who had ridden many winds, was wondering at their speed they set him down among the crags and whirled away. He was stumbling between rocks and sank down on one of them to rest.

He had come over more than half the land, catching up with the sun. He would not choose to be spirit-carried oftener than he must; he sat feeling only the turning of the world that was like stillness, and its quiet that was like the deep quiet of thought.

At last he saw that he was in a gully under steep walls of rock. It was shadowed and cool though sunlight fell down its farther wall; a wisp of grey mist drifted in it and was gone. He knew that Balyet, killer of children, must be near, and since death had refused her she must still be human; but he saw no sign. He went up the gully a little way to look but came back and sat down again. It was safer to wait where the Jannoks had left him. At last he grew impatient and shouted to her: "Balyet!"

At once the gully was alive and full of calling: "Balyet—Balyet—Balyet!" And it seemed to Wirrun that the voice could not be his own thrown back by the rocks. It was a softer voice full of something he could not name. Where he had only called, this voice now yearned. A trail of mist curled over his feet and drifted away up the gully.

Frowning he called again. And again, first here then there, the voice pleaded back: "Balyet—Balyet—Balyet—" With his hand on the power he saw that she was there, the woman who could not die; she fled up the gully and drifted down again.

She was so thinned by time that he barely saw her, scarcely more than a voice that cried back to others and her shadow no more than a trail of mist. Her shape was not old or young but only a woman's, wind-drifting. What he saw was the shadowed darkness of her eyes. He saw those dark shadows of longing and loneliness and he knew why she folded the children in her arms, and how she must wail with grief when they quietly died. He was filled with pity for this long punishment.

He saw her float unresting up the gully and come drifting down again. He thought the dark eyes fixed on him with sudden eagerness and that that was why he felt chilled; but then he saw they were fixed on something behind him, and he turned his head rigidly and looked.

There was the thing: a white shadow without shape or warmth or life, a wreathing of mist behind him. And though it had no eyes he knew it watched.

He had not guessed that the woman would follow the death so close. He had lit no fire.

4

The thing that was called Noatch lay like a patch of mist
in the gully and watched. And even with his hand on the
power Wirrun was afraid: it was as though a blind man
watched. The mist curled and wreathed and changed, there
was no shape to Noatch. It thinned into nothing and thick-
ened into mist, the blind watcher never wholly seen. He
knew from its ancient cold denial of life that the thing had
no speech. It was a slow thing yet it had the speed to catch
a flying spirit. As the Jugi had its monster-smell of dog so
this thing had the monster-smell of fear and Wirrun was
afraid.

Then the shade of Balyet flowed past him entreating; a
woman as he was a man, and pleading to be denied life. In a
flash the blind watcher was gone, leaving her to drift away
down the gully with a wind-cry of despair. And again Wirrun was angry. He could not change the fate of Balyet; no
man or hero could do that. But anger warmed him and called
him back to life.

He was no naked helpless spirit seeking its home—he was
a living man. If Noatch had any power over him let the
power be seen. He was here at the call of earth-things and
had faced worse things than this one. He had come to draw
it near and watch it: to see if its refusal of one sad spirit
gave it power over others and the right to call itself a death.
He would not be put off because the thing instead had
watched him. Tight-lipped he looked for fuel for a fire to
draw it back.

He was reaching for a stick when again its dank cold reached him. It had come without drawing.

He straightened and turned. It lay along the high rocks of the gully like a mist dissolving at the edges and it watched. He went back to where he had left his pack and sat down; leaning against the rock, he watched too. He thought grimly that maybe this would unsettle the brute; it was more used to terror than to watching.

Yet it seemed a useless waste of time. He had seen already that Noatch had no likeness to the fire-eyed thing that had looked at him with menace, and watching it he could see nothing more. If there were questions to ask he could not frame them or Noatch answer them, even if it would. Still he looked, lying carelessly back on the rocks, and soon he saw there were other earth-things near it.

They were often hidden but always appeared again: man-shaped things, grey-haired and emu-footed like those that had brought him. Now and then they glanced at Wirrun with sharp, calculating looks, but always they watched Noatch and kept their places near it as it shifted and writhed. He thought they must follow and watch over it, and that such a thing would need these followers—creatures to give life to its denial of life.

And certainly these others could speak. If he had questions to ask he could ask them of these Jannoks . . . except that he knew they would not answer. He remembered the words of Ko-in.

Ask for no knowing or searching or doing . . . but ask for yourself what you need.

He'd do more than ask, he thought irritably. He'd make them answer if he could. His need was to know. He looked again at Noatch.

It drifted, twisted, changed and was the same, the blind watcher half-seen. Shapeless, colourless, warmthless . . . drawn to fire because it had no warmth . . . Drawn to colour, then, because it had no colour?—to shape because it had no shape? There was his billy, strapped to his pack: that was a shape. Almost idly Wirrun began to think. While he did it he sat up and fumbled carelessly with his pack. He could still feel a dank cold coming from above.

He had decided that the circle of the billy was a shape too natural and unending to draw a thing that curled like mist. A circle was the sky, a tree-trunk, a nest, the sun. Noatch had the land's great burning sun to warm it, a sun that cracked rock; but it came to a little man-made fire. He needed an unnatural shape, something straight-sided and sharp-cornered . . . He had one of the straps of his pack unbuckled; he reached into a pocket and drew out the red-lacquered box.

He played with it for a while, turning it this way and that. The hard bitter thing inside him stirred quickly but he would not let it grow into pain; he thought as quickly of Balyet and let his anger turn towards Noatch. He thought of the mirrors that lined the box and wondered if they might be useful. He remembered that Noatch was used to men's terror; it would hardly expect an invitation.

He shuffled his feet a little, looking for smoother rock; reached for a dead twig and carelessly chewed it; opened and closed the box, flashing its mirrored lid. At last he bent forward and set it down close by his left big toe, and while his body covered it, propped its lid slightly open on one end of the twig. The other end he pushed between his toes. Then he lay back in his old position and let his eyelids droop.

The box stood alone, straight-sided and sharp-cornered on rough rock. The sun that spilt into the gully lit its red to brilliance. Looking down between his knees Wirrun could see it there; looking sideways he could see up and down the gully. He could not see Noatch above him but soon he felt its cold increase. Yet he knew from an excited chittering of Jannoks that it was in the same place.

At little time went by. Wirrun kept his eyelids lowered and his ears alert. He heard the Jannoks twitter from farther to his right, and then from lower down. They seemed alarmed. He strained his eyes to the right, up the gully, and watched its rocky floor.

The white mist flowed into a hollow of rock and lay floating there, cupped and restless. The Jannoks moved about it crooning and coaxing. Sometimes it licked quickly at their claw-toed feet so that they chittered and leapt back. Its coldness rolled nearer: it lay against a rock close by. Wirrun lay still.

It moved again; it flowed over and around the box while the Jannoks uttered warning cries and Wirrun felt a cold sweat on his ankles. A wisp of Noatch curled under the lid— in a flash it was gone—inside the box? Wirrun, startled, jerked his foot hard. The lid of the box cracked shut and he jammed his foot down on it quickly. The Jannoks screamed in fury.

"I reckon I might give this to Balyet," said Wirrun sitting up with his hand on the power and his foot on the box. "Or will I take it north with me?" A huge cold anger came through the lid of the box and chilled his foot, but he thought the mirrors might confuse the thing for a while.

"Die! You must die!" shrieked the Jannoks.

"A good time for it," said Wirrun, "while the big boss is shut up safe and can't get after me. But you tell me a bit about that other death, the one up north, and I might let this one out."

"We tell you nothing, big-head!" they screamed. "That thing is your affair. Let the death out!"

Wirrun laughed. "You told me one thing already—this is no death." His leg was aching to the knee with cold. "Maybe it's your big boss but it's not mine. This thing can be fooled. A man can draw it off with a fire or shut it up in a box. What sort of death is that?"

They glowered at him and reached for the box. He dragged it closer and his hand was always on the power.

"What about this other one up north? Is that a real death —better than this misty-looking thing?"

They spat at him. "That rubbish. A man has made it.

But good enough for you, big-head. You will not shut that one up in a box."

"You never know," said Wirrun.

They sneered at him. One of them said, "Can you fool a thing made of your own worst parts? Your knowing of evil, your power, your greed, your fear—" The others stirred and muttered and that one fell silent.

"Hum," said Wirrun. "The best of me'll just have to be a match for the worst of me, won't it? What do I call this thing when I see it?"

Even that they refused to answer till he changed feet on the box like a man settling down to wait. Then they muttered, "Wulgaru."

"All right," said Wirrun, since he could think of nothing else to ask. He drew the power out of its bag and laid the fur-wrapped stone for a moment on the lid of the box. "Now I'll leave this box here while I climb out of this place, and when I'm gone you can open it. It won't open till then." He stood up, looking down at the box with a darkened face. "Tell your boss he can have it. Present from the Ice-Fighter."

They watched angrily while he strapped his pack, heaved it on and began to climb out of the gully. "Do not die in this country, Hero," they called after him. "Noatch will run fast for you."

"That's friendly," said Wirrun, and he climbed up into the sunlight to warm himself and rest; for though he had reached another place where he could not stay he had not found any purpose that called him on and had no wish for another spirit-journey.

He found a mountain slope studded with box trees, warm in the sun of mid-afternoon and looking wide over grassed plains below. He was not hungry but made a small fire and brewed tea, for his legs ached with the cold of Noatch and all his body was chilled. When the tea was made he let the fire die and sat drinking tea and sun together. He felt cold and weary in every bone, and a bitter sadness he could no longer hide from; and somewhere, somehow, a secret touch of comfort.

He had known before he saw Balyet that the law had no pity. He had known before he saw Noatch that death was no cold, blind spirit-chaser that a man could fool; that it was as the People said, an end and a beginning. He had proved no more than this and could not tell where the comfort came from.

His mind went back to Ularra, whose story he had told to the men of the Centre. No death and no spirit-chaser had caught that spirit, he knew; it had escaped from the ancient dark into the rustle of leaves and the whisper of grass. And it came to Wirrun that of the two of them, himself and Ularra drawn by the singing of the silver water-spirit, Ularra had chosen the better way.

FOUR

In the Country of the Yunggamurra

I

Of all his journeys the one to the north was most like a dream in Wirrun's mind. He called for it late at evening when the old sense of restless dissatisfaction had grown strong—when he must move somewhere and knew no other way to go. He was at once seized by a great man thing whose head was hidden in shaggy white hair and beard so that only its eyes and nose could be seen, was thrust into a bag and hoisted to the creature's shoulder, and after that knew little more than speed and darkness.

He was brought out of the bag into starlit darkness and the smell of marsh, and was caught up again and carried for a long time through water. He felt only its silken tugging and sometimes the rougher grasp of weed and the suck of mud. Those who carried him seemed women from the waist up, but their legs were the legs of great frogs. Sometimes the darkness grew thick and close and the water's lapping rang hollow, and he knew they travelled by underground rivers; and so at last they reached a billabong whose shores dulled and glowed like a fire. When the frog-women drew him towards this glow he saw them clearly for the first time: their faces were as lovely as their large webbed feet and splayed and leathery knees were ugly.

A crowd of little men were gathered on the shore—he glimpsed long ears, big heads and bellies carried on stick-thin legs and saw that the ground of all that country glowed like fire. But the little men bore him fast, laid like a log along their shoulders, and soon he saw only the blur of leaves and stars and after that nothing at all.

It was still night when he felt grass under him where he lay under a great broad dome of sky pierced with stars. The lights of a car flashed by on some road not far away. He waited, dazed, but no earth-thing came; only something small and furry, warm with life, blundered against his foot and scurried off. He roused himself to pull out his sleeping-bag and crawled into it and slept heavily until morning.

Then he found he was lying in tall brown grass with polished stems that glistened in the early sun. A straggle of box trees and bloodwood crouched low on the plain to his left; behind him the dark green heads of native plum and the white railing of a bridge marked the line of some creek or river. The sky was still a broad, full dome, now blue. He knew only that he had asked to be set down "somewhere near Katherine" and the town could not be far away. He could think of nothing to do except to look for some breakfast. He had finished Tom Hunter's chops last night at the white-misted mountains.

He stowed his pack in a patch of grevillea, took his water-bag and went down to the river. It was a small stream but flowing well and its water tasted sweet. He filled his bag and walked along the bank looking for a deeper pool hidden from the road. On the way he found the trailing green of yams and dug several large tubers. He reached a pool well screened by banks and trees and stripped off and slid quietly in: if there were fish he knew he could catch them.

He caught two unfamiliar catfish under the banks, killed them and laid them by his canvas bag, washed the yams and himself, dried off in the sun and dressed. And all this time, though the river ran so quietly, he was haunted by a sound that he could not quite hear but that he thought was the calling of water.

He carried his breakfast back to the bark-littered ground under the straggling box trees, fetched his pack, lit a small fire and while it built its coals cleaned his fish and set stones to heat. Often he grew still to listen for some far-off waterfall and shook his head with irritation when he heard nothing but birds.

When he had eaten and repacked he sat impatiently wondering what to do now. He had arrived at the place he had chosen, in a country at least near the country of the thing he had been called on to find. What next? He had no plan to approach it, or to seek some power he might use against it; he had so far only resisted and avoided it and did not ask himself, even now, why he had come or why he did nothing. He only felt impatiently that he must do something next— and that here he was too close to the road for freedom—and that beyond this point he knew nothing of the country he was in. He took up his pack and began to walk.

He walked up the river, keeping it in sight since it was water and food in a strange land. It led him closer to looming cliffs of rock, yellow in the sun, ragged and scantily tree-clad, that seemed to wall the plain. He remembered that these would be outlying arms of the escarpment, the worn and broken edges of the high rock-country that was near. The wide-skied, tall-grassed, rock-bared country of the north soothed him as the quiet Centre did. Sometimes he stood still, losing while he listened for it the half-heard sound of falling water.

By late afternoon those walls of rock had closed in to east and west on the river. He had walked a long way under the pressure of the northern heat and was tired and ready to camp. And except that he had recognised the escarpment he knew no more of the country than he had when he began.

He remembered that far away in the east this red-eyed thing, this Wulgaru, had obeyed his power when he met it. In a moment of exasperation, perhaps with himself, he gripped the stone and called aloud: "Come on, you Wulgaru. I'm calling you."

Nothing happened. Remembering how it had lain hidden he set down his pack and went searching among scrub and rocks. He could find no trace of it: whatever the thing had done in the east it had not obeyed his power here. That shook him into thinking for a while.

He thought slowly while he chose a place to camp, caught more fish, this time with a line, set snares that he baited with raw fish, filled his water-bag and billy, gathered wood and made his fire. By then he had concluded that it would have served him right if he had succeeded in calling up trouble while he was tired and hungry and had no clear idea of where he was, or whether the thing he sought was in reach of his power, or even if he was in the right country.

While his meal cooked he argued that he was not going to find out much more about the country by crawling over it like a fly—or, judging from last night, carried at the speed of earth-things. He needed to see it fast and wide by his own means, and he had the means. And what was that cursed sound he couldn't hear?

While he ate he considered his means of travelling fast and wide, and tried to prepare his mind. It was a dangerous means, and especially in a strange country; but he had been given the whole of the land for his country; this country too was his.

In this land of burning distances his ancestors had lived for unknown ages; he was not the first who had needed to travel it farther and faster than a man can walk. His People had long ago learnt the way: to free their spirits in sleep. To travel in the spirit as a man does in dreaming and return to their sleeping bodies when the journey was done. It was a way to be taken only at need—to leave the body empty, unprotected, while the spirit went naked and at risk among others stranger and darker than itself. But Wirrun had done it once before.

When his meal was over he banked his fire between stones and drew over it ash and charcoal for safety and warmth while he slept. While he did this he tried to still his spirit to that deep aching pain, and his mind to thought and anger and doubt of Ko-in. He sat for some time holding between his hands the power wound in its cord, letting his hands feel it while his spirit reached out to feel the night: dark, moonless, with that star-pierced dome enclosing it and mischief stirring in it and shy things hiding and others brooding deep and slow.

He climbed into his sleeping-bag and lay with his hands still folded on the stone and his spirit still reaching for the whisper of grasslands and rivers and the strong proud silence of stone; and he said to them in his spirit, "I am here. All countries are mine. I claim you . . ." And he slept, and his spirit slid free and drifted up like smoke. He drifted over his sleeping body, a shadow of himself holding a shadow of the stone.

And the grasslands and rivers and the high stone country were spread out for him but he could not see them. He was seized on at once by the crying of a waterfall.

It called from somewhere far off, a fall that roared and in a little while faded and in another while roared again. It was a fall that had haunted his mind for more than a year: the mysterious hush-and-fade of water out of which had come the singing of the Yunggamurra. It possessed him.

He went seeking it: first to the river he had followed all day. Hovering over it he felt the life in it, and how in the Wet it came pounding down from the plateau to the plain; but now it came only trickling and had no fall that roared and faded. He rose higher, above the broken escarpment and north over the plateau itself.

Its age came up to him like the deepest notes of an organ he had heard in a cathedral, notes that had trembled in the cathedral's stone. The deep notes of age trembled in this stone, but he listened only to the call of water. It was stronger now.

The plateau was square-cut with joints, each deeply carved and tree-lined, each a river interlocked with others. He slid over great gorges in which trickling streams grew suddenly immense and heard gentle falls that a few weeks ago had roared and shouted. He sought only a river bubbling with sly laughter and wickedness, singing both sweet and sharp like wild honey, a fall that mysteriously shouted and whispered in turn.

And he found it. High on the plateau he found it carving its way out of spring-fed marshes and over the edge of the escarpment. Its fall did not shout or whisper but sprang in smooth curves from ledge to ledge till it ribboned down a long drop into the valley; but its hushing voice was the one that had called out of the old enchantment. Hovering over it he felt its slyness and its nurturing of ancient things and knew it with certainty. He had found the country of the Yunggamurra.

He hid among trees in case they felt his presence, and while he hung there the fall changed its note and began to fade. And his spirit fled on the breathing night. He could not look for he knew what he might see.

She was Yunggamurra now, a fragile silver thing among her sisters. He wondered with pain if he might not know her from the others—but he fled in terror that she might no longer know anything at all of him.

He sped over rocks as old as the world and over plains, not seeing where he went but only travelling fast, and the cry of a stone-curlew followed him. When he faltered and went heavily at last he thought it was because of his own terror and not from any evil in the night. He let himself sink into forest and hide among thin lancewood leaves.

Then at last he felt a darkness that was more than night and that dragged at him. He stayed close among leaves, waiting. The stone-curlew cried again. He heard wings in the darkness: not feathered wings but something strong and swooping that beat close. They came closer still—he crept deeper among leaves, and they parted, and the clumsy face with red-glowing eyes was looking at him.

If it had not come when he called, at any rate it had found his naked spirit now.

It hung like a mask among the leaves, grotesque and unmoving. Only the eyes were hard and bright and knowing, and they gazed into his. He gripped the power and drew quickly behind the cover of leaves.

A rush of air stirred the leaves as the wings swept by and circled and swept back. He waited for them to pass again, and while they turned he sped like thought to another tree-top and hid among new leaves. But the wings swept back as close as before or closer, and the leaves stirred and parted, and there hung the mask with the flame-bright eyes that looked at him.

To be hunted like this turned Wirrun's fear into anger. He held up the power and cried, "Keep off! I order you!"

The face did not move but the eyes seemed to dim for a moment. He shouted his order to the swooping wings, holding up the power to them, and they faltered and swept farther off. But when he turned back the eyes that a man should not see were flame-bright and staring again, and while he threatened the face with his power the wings swept back.

His anger blazed. With the power in his left hand he seized the mask-face with his right and turned it so that he need not see it. It screamed when he touched it and burnt like fire, but he was still himself, and the wings beat in fear, and the face felt as it had looked—a wooden mask, hollowed and empty. And since he should not look at it and would not let it go he held it like a mask before his own face and looked through its flame-bright eyes.

At once he saw the troops of dark wings like giant bats, and the spirits of dead men drifting and wailing below, and the land's dark mass spread out in rain-carved heights and valleys and swamps, and star-flecked rivers snake-gliding to the sea; but the dead were cowed weak things that had failed in life, and the land was wearing into nothing, and the rivers hid old and fearful things. He felt a bitter hardness that was not his own, and under it an anger that was his and fought to be free; and he clung with all his strength to the stone of power.

He came out of the treetops, masked behind the face, and

the bat-wings swept beside him and the spirits wailed and followed; and the rustling night grew still as he passed. He let his own anger carry him back to his camp with the fire banked down and his body safely sleeping. Slender curious spirits of rocks and caves drifted about it, and fled when they saw the mask come through the dark.

He went quickly to his fire and uncovered it and dropped the mask in. It screamed again and vanished, gone without burning. Wirrun shivered and slid quickly into his body. For a moment he felt it enclose him: the weight that pressed him into his sleeping-bag, the beat of his pulse, the cool, even flow of air in his lungs, and in his hands the softness of fur that wrapped the hardness of the stone of power. In the next moment he slept.

2

Wirrun slept only fitfully and woke before daylight, hearing clearly now the half-heard sound of yesterday. He remembered his spirit-flight looking through the fiery knowing eyes of the thing that called itself death and thrust the memory away with a shiver and an uneasy look at his right hand. The hand was not withered or damaged; its flesh had not held the mask-face. And after all his long journeys in search of this thing he felt only a smouldering anger that it had hunted him. His ears were filled with the calling of the Yunggamurra's river.

He lay in his sleeping-bag waiting for the sun, and the trouble inside him was no longer a stone but something that swelled and churned. He longed fiercely to go in his body to the river and to see it with his eyes, but he fought the longing and shrank from the thought of so much useless pain. His mind saw clearly that it could bring him nothing.

What could he do at the river? Only look and come away —if he were strong enough—and go on suffering as he suffered now. Could he catch her again with her sisters at hand and smoke her again into a golden girl? Maybe: and what then? At best a few more weeks of troubled, uncertain happiness, and after that—all of it over again. He clenched his hands. How many times could a man go through that gain and loss?

Or how many years could he live at the call of a river?

There must be a way—or how could she have come to him in the first place knowing what she knew? How could anything do that to a man?—how could Murra? By her own words she had known what must happen. He was flooded with memories of her playing in the water—swinging high in a tree—throbbing with delight on the wind—running over unbending grass and sitting distrustful by the fire with her dark hair stirring; of her coaxing and teasing, the tenderness of her singing and the courage of her laughter. Oh Murra— water-girl—could you do that to a man? There must be some other way.

And he saw that there was another way. There was Ularra's way.

He fingered the thought, and in a moment a feverish excitement took hold of him. That was the way: to stop running, stop suffering and require of her Ularra's peace. He would go in his body to the country of the Yunggamurra and see it with his eyes; and she who had known the end at the beginning would press him under the water with her long nails and give him that strong calm peace she had given to Ularra. She would remember; even slimed with the silver of the Yunggamurra she would know what she did. He would not think that now she might have forgotten and would drown him like another man.

He thought instead with the fever mounting that now his body must travel to the river, and his burdened restless spirit knew the way, and the river called. He thought he could find it in a couple of days of hard walking—or in a moment if he called for earth-things to carry him. But his troubled spirit rebelled at that; as soon as the grey light was strong enough he began to prepare for the walk.

Pleased with his calm good sense he caught fish for breakfast and more to take with him wrapped in a wet shirt; for a man must eat if he wants to walk hard under the pressure of the northern sun. He dug more yams and collected his empty snares; made his fire, cooked and ate breakfast, filled his water-bag and rolled his pack. As the sun was rising he set out to find a road, for his spirit had seen that a road was near.

He struck first a track and then a highway north-east along

the plain. He walked it for most of the day with the sound of the river in his ears. He saw none of the speeding traffic till a grey van overtook him and the driver, a man of the People with a face pock-marked with old scars, offered him a lift. It was a silent drive for the driver too was a silent man; but sometimes he cast a sidelong look at the haunted figure beside him.

When they reached a town Wirrun thanked him briefly and climbed out listening for the river. The drive had saved him a day's walk but he could get farther on before night; he chose a road north. At dark he camped where he was on a hillside, relying on the water he carried. The crying of the river was clearer now. Through the exhaustion of the day and the heat he felt a hard triumph, and he climbed into his sleeping-bag and slept.

But he slept badly. Whenever his mind sank deep enough to loose its hold his troubled spirit struggled to get free on some business of its own. Again and again he was jerked awake, dreaming of bat-wings or drowning and hearing the waterfall rush and fade. Towards morning he slept more deeply and woke late at last in full sunlight. The river was still calling. He ached and did not ask whether it was in mind or body or spirit.

Doggedly he ate and drank and rolled his pack. Doggedly he walked and listened. He was soon finished with roads and followed fainter and fainter tracks, and sometimes blundered through trackless shining grass that hid logs and rocks and for all he knew snakes, or through low straggling forest where the trees posed awkwardly and his feet crunched on thin curled sheddings of bark. Sometimes as he stumbled on he talked to his dead friend.

"Only her, mate . . . none of those others . . . she'll know me all right."

"Peace, mate, a man's gotta have peace."

"No good to a man . . . a bit of slime, you said."

The call of the waterfall was clear and even, hushing gently in the heat. The sun had gone down when he stopped short knowing that he heard it with his ears and not only from within. The fever of excitement rose strongly and called back his mind.

He looked for the fringe of trees that would show him the river so that he could follow it up to the fall—but a stab of cunning stopped him from making that mistake. He put his hand on the power and thought more clearly: they would feel him near, he must keep away from the river. He was going of his own choice to the one Yunggamurra who would hold him under the water with her long nails—oh yes, she'd remember, she'd know. He would not be drawn against his will to the whole band of sisters.

He looked instead for the line of the escarpment, moving the net bag on his belt to keep the power between him and the river. He reached the fall at dusk and quickly unwound a length of grey-fur cord and laid it in a wide circle near the river. He stayed within the circle.

The fall hushed steadily on, still bright in the dusk. His spirit knew it well and curled and cringed somewhere near his belly but he did not feel it. He sat on a boulder within a screen of leaves and watched the water build its unchanging curves at the lip of the fall, spring in its smooth leap over rocks halfway down and fall in plumes into the pool below. Already, in watching it, he found a kind of peace and reached for his water-bag and drank. Dusk brightened into young moonlight and the water gleamed.

A moment came when he gripped the power and grew tense: into the hush of water had come a sound that rang like drops in a cave and he knew it was laughter. It led his straining eyes to the lip of the fall and in a little while he saw them: a gleam of silver limbs and a shine of dark hair in the light of the young moon.

He saw them gathered above the fall, a line of them across the river. They were laughing as they twined their arms together and laid themselves across the flow. The hush of the waterfall changed, faded, its gleaming curves flattened and its plumes wavered and fell; there was only a whisper of water. Above it the laughter grew, the line of silver bodies strained and struggled, their dark hair washed over their shoulders as the water behind them mounted and trickled past. Suddenly the straining line broke—hung wavering—and on a leap and roar of released water the Yunggamurra came spinning and tumbling over the fall into the pool below. The waterfall built its curves again and hushed steadily on.

He had seen what made it mysteriously roar and fade and the pain was like a blunt stone knife, for he had seen the game before. Fierce and proud and enduring she had played her sisters' game alone; one Yunggamurra sitting between stones in the trickle of a tiny creek, letting herself be carried a foot or so down into a pool and never speaking of what she remembered.

When he recovered he saw that the sisters had climbed the wet rocks of the fall and reformed their line at the top. He crouched in leaf-shadow in the circle of the power and fingered the tightness of waiting as a fisherman fingers his line. The voice of the fall softened as its water fell. Above it the laughter bubbled and rang and the Yunggamurra twined and struggled to hold to each other and their eyes shone like stars. The line strained, broke, wavered on a wall of water, and was flung in a debris of moonlit gleams down into the pool. With the power in his hands he sprang forward and shouted before they could flash away.

"Wait! Stay!"

She would know him, she would know—

All their startled faces turned to him. In a moment they were huddled on rocks on the far side of the pool—but they were ordered and could not go. A hero with a power had come on them and the proud Yunggamurra lifted their heads and howled. He saw their sharp claws scratch at rock like angry crabs, and their gleaming throats pulse and their dark wet hair twine about them. They were all as lovely and dangerous as moonlight and water and he could not tell one from another.

"Where is she?" he shouted. "The one you brought back in the storm. The one that was with me."

The howling died and they turned to him all their indifferent faces, all their old, moonlit eyes. The moment built into a wave like the one they had built in the river.

"Murra!" he shouted. "You know me whatever you are. Come out of that, girl!" They gazed at him. "Where is she?" he roared.

They answered at last in cold sharp-sweet voices. "Gone. She is lost and gone."

Seven—he knew there should be seven—feverishly he counted them. There were six.

"Gone? Lost? How lost? You took her back!"

Their eyes were indifferent, absent. "We do not know how or where. We cannot sense her. She is gone and lost."

The moment broke and crashed over him. He stumbled away from the river and left them: the proud Yunggamurra defeated but untaken, shamed. Their howling followed him and grew fainter, and at last he fell into a thicket to lie.

The moment had flowed away and left him stranded.

She was gone; the land kept its inexorable laws. Ularra's way was not allowed to him. He saw at last he had not come in love and despair seeking peace, but only in anger and seeking revenge; dragged there by no enchantment but his own.

3

They were clever and cunning, her sisters. They clung about her in the wildness of the storm, entangled and bound her in their hair, enmeshed her in arms and legs and filled her ears with singing of her lost river-country. They carried her down into streams and leapt up again in new storms. They bathed her in mud till her skin softened and paled, till her silver slime grew again and tiny leeches crept back into her pores. From storm to river and river to storm they brought her across the land, and sang with joy of the lost Yungga-murra found and how far they had travelled—farther than in all the ages—to bring her home. There was laughter and singing wherever she turned, there was always a slime-soft hand in hers and an arm about her waist till at last, as in the old days, she could not rest alone. And so, in a short time at the speed of earth-things, they had her back.

She sank with them into her own remembered river. There were the great yellow cliffs standing over it, and the palm and plum and wild passionfruit hanging. Its water was softer than any, its fish sweet and lively, its waterfall leapt and called. Under quiet banks the tresses of weed moved together like voices in song. Combing her hair with her long clawed nails she wondered how she had lived so long away: how it was that she had not broken like a bubble or dried into dust with loneliness for her sisters and longing for her dear and only river. For they were herself and they made her real.

It was a thing she could wonder in the midst of a water-game, while her laughter joined with the others and her voice called or sang with theirs. She did not wonder alone for she could never bear to be alone. That was a darkness, and silence was a danger on the edge of it. Her sisters knew it too: they were never apart and never let the silence hang —except sometimes for a moment, looking at her. Then, when she hurried to break the silence that she could not bear, there were secret knowing glances and a tiny smile passing from mouth to mouth.

One day, seeing that, she broke off the song she had begun and let the silence creep back for a moment while she looked at her sisters. How many had been taken as she had, and turned with smoke and taught to know tenderness? She could not remember, the ages were so long, but she knew some had. Was that how they learnt the danger of silence and the darkness of being alone? Was that why their smiles were small? She had no time to think about it then, for the silence grew too long for the others and they broke it with a game; but she let the thought lie in her mind.

There came a day when all the water-games were played and the sisters looked for a new one. Then again they glanced at her and the little smiles went from mouth to mouth. One of them cried, "I know a game! Quickly, bring me a white stone!" and she gave the Yunggamurra a little push. So the Yunggamurra dived quickly to find a white stone, and when she brought it back the others were gone. They had left her alone.

And first she called them in fear but they did not come, and then she flashed to and fro to look for them, chattering empty words to keep the silence away. But the darkness was pressing closer, the darkness of being alone; and suddenly it pounced and caught her, and it was shaped like a great dark cavern with a glint of water in it. The Yunggamurra stopped her frantic search and was still, for she knew that cavern. She had been alone before: long alone, and in a very deep old dark. In her stillness she sank, and the river washed her under its banks and she lay there and let memory wash her too.

It could not be for long for her sisters would not let her win their game and came to find her, calling in anxious voices and smiling little smiles. But memory runs fast and she had time enough to learn what darkness lay beyond the edge of silence. It was sorrow.

After that she learnt to play a secret game of her own: to slip away for a moment between rocks and laugh when she was found—to tumble and spin a little longer in the waterfall and climb a little slower to the top, to play and sing with the rest and yet to be alone; to gather moments. And if she kept the memory close every moment brought her something.

Sometimes it was the beauty that the land hid under its rocks, the secret sparkle of stone. Sometimes it was the shimmer of the eastern sea or a glimpse of dark faces dreaming while she sang. Most often it was one dark face, sober with care but breaking into the warmth of a smile; memories flew like leaves in the wind about that face. Once, with a slash of pain, she saw it darkened with loss and staring up into storm.

Once a moment brought a question: did her sisters who had been taken play this secret game as she did? Watching she did not think so; they kept the group whole as if each truly lived in the others. They sank or rose, sang or played as one, and only she was a fraying at the edge of the group. She could not know how it came about that she was changed from every Yunggamurra of them all: that in all the ages of their being—free in the river or taken to the dry world and taught to know tenderness—only she had been shut away alone a long time and learnt to know herself. She had learnt while the land held her shut in its great fist with the pale spiders and ancient crumbling bones. For others too there were lost faces and sorrow waiting to pounce. For her there was also herself.

She had never time for such thinking but little by little

she gathered materials for thought. In an age or two, perhaps, she might have threaded the moments together into thought. They only tumbled through her mind like a handful of pebbles on the day the man came with the gun.

On that day all the Yunggamurra were in the pool above the fall. They were restless and tense and did not play, for they heard the crack of the rifle and the shrieking and crying of birds and knew there were men about. They heard these sounds often: it need not mean that the oldest game, the Yunggamurra game, was beginning. The men might not come near the river, or they might be too many, or white men. It need not mean that the game was beginning—but it might.

The bad old game of the Yunggamurra did not come often in these days. Their hunger for it kept them sharp-eyed, waiting. They heard the rifle-crack high on the escarpment: he had climbed! He would go to the marsh for the water-birds, and that was near! They quivered and grew still. He came closer; they could sense that this was truly one man alone, a man of the People. Their sharp eyes softened and glowed. The one who had been lost quivered and tensed as eagerly, softened and glowed as cunningly, as they all did. It was the game!

With the others she drew herself on to the rocks and sat languid and lovely combing her hair. Her voice yearned as sweetly as theirs in the drifting notes of the old love-singing. She softened her smile and lit her eyes as they did, and swayed to the singing and longed for him to come.

Are you not coming?

He heard, was caught, came nearer; they drew him on. Their voices had never been so sweet and magic.

And then the moments of memory went tumbling through her mind and she saw in the river the shadow of a drowned face and heard her own voice crying *your friend is between us!* And the man came closer and she knew she would not drown him.

Still she sang and swayed a little longer, for this was her

dear and only river and her sisters' life was hers. They saw the man among the trees, they all leaned forward in longing, and quietly she slid into the water like a ripple and let it carry her away. She did not see herself doing this or think what it meant or where it would lead. She only thought, "I will not drown him," and drifted away.

She went over the fall like foam with the singing still in her ears and was spun and tumbled into quiet water. She found a current and rode it down like a glimmer. Where two branches of the river met she turned south into the second thinking only of some place to hide—they would not easily sense her for all this water was alive with the sense of Yunggamurra, but they were swift and cunning finders. She knew a small crack between rocks where she had sometimes stolen a few of her secret moments. She found it and slipped through into a tiny dark cave: only a hollow that held a puddle of stale water from the Wet. She huddled in it.

And now she had more moments than she had had since the First Dark and she began to think. And first she saw that of all the Yunggamurra sisters only she could stay so long in this silent lonely place. And next she saw that she could not refuse the Yunggamurra game and still return to her sisters; she would be forced to play it another time.

Then she saw quite suddenly that after all there had been a sort of choice and she had made it: not between earth-spirit and woman for that choice was not hers, but between her secret self and all that was sweet for a Yunggamurra. Slipping over the waterfall she had slipped away forever. Where should she go?

She might find a way into the deep caverns where she had been lost before, and learn to bear again the First Dark and the land's old bitter water . . . Or in the cool night she might travel over land and find some water where no old thing lived—some place where deep rocks had moved and a spring broken through. But in every country she must pass she would be an intruder, out of her place and in danger; she must always watch.

It was a hard thing, to choose her secret self and be alone . . .

She chose to travel over the land at night; and if she could find no new water she might find a road deep into rock. When a bright-polished moon hung in the sky she climbed quickly out of the river and began her journey.

She travelled easily at first. The ground was hard to her mud-soft feet, sticks and twigs scraped at her protective slime, but the Wet was not long over and the waters were still many. She easily found small waterholes in which no old thing lived and in which she could lie by day and be healed. There were still frogs in plenty, and small fish and water-beetles and weed; she was not hungry. In spite of that, land-travel was not her kind of travelling and the distances were great. She went slowly, circling in search of some water that was not linked to her own river or the rivers of others, that was not inhabited by any old thing like herself, that would out-last the Dry.

She was very lonely—a small silver thing that crawled over the vastness of the land and had no time to play; but she had been lonely in a darkness without moon or stars or shadowy trees and she bore it. She was often afraid and remembered how to hide.

The shy Mimi who lived within the rocks did not worry her. Though they saw that she wandered they avoided her as she avoided them, and frowned at a distance or retreated into rock. The small powerful Podji-Podji over whose underground homes she trespassed were only curious; they were free of the sunlight and not angered by a water-spirit straying at night. But the Nabeado water-girls drove her furiously from their river; the Mormo of the caves were of many kinds and not to be trusted; and she often sensed older, darker powers strange to her, and knew too well that she must not meet them.

South over plains she went, circling and searching. Once or twice she thought she had found a way down underground to the old water, but when she sank into it this water was too hot and bitterly stinging for her. And the days went by and the small surface waters began to dwindle and dry.

South and east were the dry lands where she could not live. North was her own country from which she fled. The Yunggamurra turned west.

Almost at once she sensed her own river that had turned south and west too. That made it harder to keep to her purpose, harder to spend a day in the mud of a shallow lagoon under water-lilies. For one day she weakened and sought her river: it brought news of her sisters far away upstream, and she knew it carried news of her downstream away from them. She rested and recovered and ate sweet fish, and yet she could not sleep. The water tingled with knowledge of the Yunggamurra, and she had always to start up and test it in case they were too near. That day gave her strength to leave her river yet again.

And now the waters dried fast, and only a few rock-pools held. She could not travel far from those or rest safely in them and began to feel stretched and thinned, like a bubble ready to burst. There were nights when she circled aimlessly, not knowing what purpose drove her on.

So it was that one dawn she found herself on the bank of a small drainage dam that held only a puddle. Uncertain which way to turn she slipped wearily into the puddle to rest awhile; and when the sun was strong and the water turned to mud she woke in despair. There was no water near that she knew. She looked hopelessly about and saw only a hillside of boulders where at least there was shade. She dragged herself there and crept into shadows between boulders and slept exhausted.

The sun moved on. In the afternoon she lay in sunlight on rock and did not feel it; the bubble was stretched very thin. Though her ear was pressed to the rock she did not hear sounds within it: a deep *boom-boom* or a strange high humming that rose and fell. The last of her grey slime dried and fell away in strips. A million tiny leeches wriggled out of her pores and were shrivelled on the rocks. In another moment she would dry into dust.

But in that moment a strange figure came out of the hill: a figure like a man half-crouched, with a sharp and beaky nose and with eyes screwed up against the light. It lifted the frail Yunggamurra in its arms and carried her into the hill, humming as it went like the wind in long grass and walking *boom-boom* through deep dark caverns. And though she was almost dust the Yunggamurra stirred and moved her dry lips, for the stuff of which she was made felt a presence very old and very great. And the shy kind spirit, He-of-the-Long-Grass, went booming and humming along his hidden ways: sharp-nosed and crouching—forgotten and discarded by men—and richly beautiful.

She woke in a pool of sweet water that came trickling in a stream through caverns. There was daylight, but dim and cool; it came through a pot-hole above where twisted roots gripped the rock. She looked and felt and slept again. The next time she woke she saw cakes of ground grass-seed left on the rocks above the pool. She looked at them in awe; for she was a Yunggamurra who had drowned men but he whose vibrations filled the cavern had fed and cared for men while they remembered him. She was awed that his pity should extend to her but she ate a little and slept again.

In a few days she was strong enough to take up the task of living alone: here, in this one pool that He-of-the-Long-Grass had given her. She would not follow the trickling stream up or down; the small fish that darted through her fingers and away down the stream, the spider or lizard that scuttled off into the dark, had escaped into sanctuary for she would not take more than she was given. Sometimes she caught the vibration of booming footsteps or a humming voice and lay still. Sometimes when all the rocks seemed quiet she sang a little, of memories or great rivers or of herself alone.

She saw that she was golden again: her silver slime had gone and there was no rich mud to bring it back. "In time it will come again," she murmured.

At night she often climbed through the pot-hole to feel the wind and the dark spreading land and to look at stars. In time she ventured far enough on the surface of the land to gather figs and a little wild honey and a moth or two. Once she found yams and dug them excitedly and took them back to her cavern; only then did she realise with disgust that they were raw and too hard to eat.

"I can make fire," she said—and sat astonished listening to the words; thinking of the play and shift of red-and-yellow light in her cavern, of a dark face lost and the warmth and company of fire. But she did not make it. To the Yunggamurra fire and smoke are a choking fear. She buried the yams in the soil again.

One night she sat in a tree above her pot-hole in the rustle and sway of wind, looking wide over the land by moonlight while the wind billowed the long shining grass. She was singing of the land that was old by day and young by night, when suddenly she quivered and was still. The wind brought a tingle of knowledge that took away her breath and all her strength: she could not believe it and she could not move.

But it was true, he was near and the wind brought him nearer, he who was at the core of all her memories, whose brown face looked upward in the storm. He could not be near this hidden place on the far side of the land, but he was: his spirit, his sleeping spirit. In a flash she had slipped from her tree and into her cavern. She did not venture out again for two nights.

They had endured what had to be endured, he and she. They had been made and broken and it could not be borne again. But afterwards she made a small fire in her cavern and sat far off in a corner to watch while the dark hair moved on her shoulders. She stared hungrily till the flicker died away and left her eyes shadowed.

FIVE

The Grave-Trees

I

Wirrun, stumbling away from the howling of the water-sisters, fell into a thicket and lay there. The stars moved towards morning; in time he stirred, and sometimes rolled his head from side to side, and at last stiffly sat up. He was dusty, red-eyed, stubble-chinned. He had driven himself hard in his pursuit of shadows. He felt beaten with whips of weariness and loss. But he was himself.

He drank, ate a little cold yam, rewound the cord of the power. Then he stood up, hoisted his pack, and by starlight began to pick his steps away from the country of the Yungga-murra.

No loss, he told himself. If she could do it . . . giving up all she'd had and loved since the land was made . . .

At some time in the night, for one fierce eager moment, he had told himself she had gone back to him: back far east to find him again. But he knew it was not true. The game was too cruel, they could never win. They were trapped in the net of old laws and old magic—but while he had sat screaming in anger and self-pity she had looked for the secret way that the net left open. He should have known it: had he not seen her, lonely and indomitable, making each place her own?

As for him, he was only a man. He could not match her, old and lovely and terrible spirit, but at least he was through with screaming. He could escape into work—instead of using it to escape only from place to place. *You have mated with magic* . . . And it had nearly destroyed him, true enough.

But Ko-in had not known its forbearance or the strength of its independence.

While he stumbled on in the starlight he turned his mind back over the way he had come. And first he remembered the echo-woman Balyet whose very shadow was faded to a wisp of mist; and he was suddenly cleanly glad of the work he had to do and of that unconquerable strength he had once named Murra. They would not fade away into an entreating mist, not himself or the silver water-spirit.

His bushman's eye, reddened and weary, still noted the escarpment looming dark against a paling sky and set a course while his mind followed another trail. The great black dog: its flowing speed and the feel of its rough hair. The old man Tom Hunter, forbearing too—*you've gone too far ahead of us, boy*. Noatch, that was all a man need fear and yet was not evil; the frog-women and the little big-ears of the fiery country. So much help, yet he had not managed to grasp his work. He had still no plan or purpose, he was still drifting.

The sun rose and began to probe down with heat. A flight of black cockatoos flashed their red tail-bands. The tall brown grass shone like silk, the stunted misshapen trees held their awkward poses. He kept to their shade when he could, rested now and then as the heat strengthened, and found the rough tracks of wheels to follow. He was thinking at last of that night when his body slept while his spirit went hunting and was hunted instead; he had not thought of it since but he shivered now to remember his flight looking though the eyes of the mask, and of how it had screamed and vanished in the fire.

In the afternoon his track became a gravelled road and brought him to some creek or river. He stayed by it during the worst of the heat: refilled his water-bag, stripped off and cooled in the stream, caught two small fish and cooked them at a tiny fire, ate and rested and thought. From time to time his ear caught the distant sound of a motor travel-

ling at speed; his road would soon bring him to the highway. This gave him a satisfaction that he had to examine
before he understood: he wanted to reach the highway before night so that he could make an early start along it tomorrow. He was going back to that camp where his body
had slept while his spirit was hunted. He had remembered
that in a game of man against spirit the man had not much
need of plan or purpose since he could not make the rules or
even know them. He could do no better than be in the right
place and meet what came, and that camp was as near as
Wirrun could come to the right place.

He would hunt again and invite another hunting, and
now that he knew it he felt stronger.

When the heat was more passive he moved on and reached
the junction with the highway before sunset. There was no
water in sight for a camp so he turned into the highway
and walked on hoping to find water before night. A car
overtook him speeding south, and a great massive low-loader
creeping and labouring north to the new mines. He walked
on the grass verge for safety and comfort.

He was frowning as he walked; his eyes watched for a
river, his ears noted the motor coming from behind, but
his mind was dark with the memory of sweeping wings and
of dead men drifting disconsolate. He did not notice the
grey van pass till it stopped ahead and then reversed back
towards him. He had only begun to see it when the pas-
senger's door swung open and the dark-skinned pock-marked
driver leaned across.

"Where to this time?" said the driver.

Wirrun stared puzzled. It took him a moment to remember
that someone had given him a lift on this road when he
travelled north, and to guess that this must be the same
driver. He nodded as though he remembered the man.

"You must live round here. I'm just looking for a camp.
Happen to know if there's water handy?"

The driver swung the door wider. "Dump your pack in

the back," and when Wirrun had climbed in and slammed the door, "There's a mudhole or two but good water's farther south. Heading far?"

"That far any rate, if you are. Thanks."

The driver nodded and started the van. Wirrun settled wearily into his seat, glad to watch the level monotonous miles flash by; glad too that the driver's jaw looked as though it were used for chewing rather than for talking. In the red glow of sunset they reached the town where last time they had parted.

"Wanta stop?" asked the man.

"Not if you're going through. Don't fancy a night in town."

The driver's jaw tightened in what might have been a smile. He had rarely seen a man less likely to enjoy a night in town. They went on south, and in the twilight the white rails of a bridge glimmered ahead.

"This do?" said the driver nodding towards the dark tree-line of the river.

"Great," said Wirrun with appreciation. "A good long start for morning. I'd never have made it." He half-turned the handle of the door waiting for the van to stop and let him out, but the driver only changed gear and swung off the roadway into long grass.

"Mind if I share it?"

Wirrun was confused for a moment. He would have preferred to camp alone, but this was a man of his People and one who had twice helped him on the road. Moreover, it began to look as though the man had driven out of his way to do it. He said, "Glad to have you," and frowned a little in embarrassment. "I got nothing much for visitors, though. I was going to do a bit of fishing."

"Too dark by the time you get bait," said the driver climbing out of the van with the key in his hand. "I got plenty." He opened the rear door, passed Wirrun his pack, took out a roll of blanket and a large battered cooler, slammed the door and headed for the fence. "Derby's the name," he said over his shoulder.

Wirrun hoisted his pack. "Thanks, Derby. Mine's—"

"I know," cut in Derby pushing his gear under tightly strained barbed wire and holding out a hand for Wirrun's pack. "Know one or two of yours," he added while he spread the wires with a hand and a foot.

"Oh." Wirrun's hand brushed the bag at his belt. "Yeah." He climbed through the wires and held them for Derby in turn, took up his pack and reached for the cooler. It slid from under his hand.

"You get that pack unrolled while you can still see," said Derby firmly. "You oughta shut them eyes or you'll bleed to death." He strode towards the shelter of the low scrub and Wirrun followed, meek and strangely shaken.

It was clear that Derby was supplying the meal and taking charge of the fire and cooking. Wirrun made the only contribution he could by bringing water from the river. Its shadowed pool and curving line seemed familiar, and so did the straggling line of a boxwood tree lit by Derby's fire. He saw that this was the place where the little big-ears had left him when they brought him north. That was luck. He had been brought to the river that was his road to the country of the red-eyed mask.

Derby, already shaking sausages in a pan, received the water with a nod of thanks. "Nice and quick," he said, referring to the sausages. "Fireplace all ready, stones and a bit of wood and all." Wirrun was heartily glad that his fireplace had speeded the cooking but he did not yet explain. After so many scrappy meals of fish and yam the smell of the sausages filled his throat, and when Derby's brown hand reached for eggs to add to them he went away abruptly to unroll his pack.

"Grub's up!" called Derby at last and Wirrun went slowly back. Two plastic plates were generously filled with sausages and eggs, another with buttered slices of bread, and the billy was in place on the fire. Derby took up his knife and fork and went to work. He did not speak or glance at Wirrun till the plates were all empty and the tea brewing. Then he ventured a sideways look and asked a question.

"Where to tomorrer?"

"Eh?" said Wirrun. He gave up the unreasonable hope of polishing his plate any cleaner with another slice of bread and answered the question. "Cross country for me from here. Up this river." He saw Derby's face grow wooden with surprise and added, "I never knew till just now. But this fireplace with the stones, that's mine; spent one night here and never saw the place from the road. You brought me luck, Derby. From here it's up this river a day's walk, in under the escarpment."

Derby poured two mugs of tea and gave another sideways glance. "In to the old graves," he said.

Wirrun's head jerked. "Old graves? I never saw any."

"Me either," said Derby. "Wouldn't want to." He settled back and blew on his tea. "The old hands know. They don't say much in case of tourists and that—there's some'd sell their own grandfather's bones for money."

"They must know too, though. Don't see how you'd keep it from any of the men of the country."

"It's all going now, old places not been used for a long time. You gotta do it right by the white man's law."

Wirrun sat drinking tea and thinking. Maybe it was all going now but he would bet that none of the men of the country would spend a night in the old burial grounds. That would be looking for trouble in the place where trouble lived; for where would a death, a spirit-stealer, live but in a burial ground?

"What's there?" he asked.

"The usual for these parts. Cave where the bones get left in the end. Bit of scrub—lancewood, I reckon—where they'd make this place up in a tree for him to lie on first."

"I know that any rate," muttered Wirrun, for his spirit had been resting in lancewood branches when its hunting began. He had drifted unknowingly into the burial trees among the helpless drifting spirits of an older dead; no wonder he was hunted. Not until Derby reached for his empty mug did he see that tidying up had begun and move to help.

"Not you," said Derby. "Into your blanket. You'll want an early start. It's near done anyhow." He had refilled the billy from a jerrycan and now poured hot water over plates and mugs. Wirrun looked on helplessly. "Get on," said Derby. "It's my stuff, I'll clean it."

That left no option. Wirrun could only mutter, "Thanks, mate. My lucky day."

"See you tomorrer," said Derby.

But Wirrun at any rate did not see him. Weary with driving himself through the heat, freed from obsession and fully fed for the first time for days, he fell at once into heavy sleep and did not wake till the sun was high. By then Derby and the grey van were gone leaving a collection of goods near Wirrun's pack: a carton of eggs, two packets of bacon, a can of baked beans and one of meat-balls, and a plastic-wrapped tray of chops. With them was a note pencilled on torn brown paper: "Cant use it dont waste it D."

Wirrun had grown unused to the luxuries of bacon and kindly despotism. He shook his head and took himself down to the river to wash and fetch water. After that he breakfasted on eggs and chops, wrapped those left over in a wet shirt buckled into a wet canvas pocket of his pack, stored the other supplies inside the pack, buried the remains of his fire, and headed up the river towards his next camp.

2

It was good to be travelling with the river again, from shade to shade under paperbark or ghost gum with the cool of the water at his right hand. At midday Wirrun stopped to brew tea and rest, his eyes wandering often to the far high shoreline of the escarpment. By sundown he came between its closing arms to the camp he remembered and found his old fireplace and brewed more tea. He sat drinking tea and looking about: he would find some heavy stones and build a cool storehouse in the river for his precious supplies; there would be fish in the river, yams along the bank, possum in the scrub. Yet he looked with tingling nerves at this good camp, for it was in the country of the evil thing and he did now know where his danger might lie.

He found himself thinking with an inward twist that Murra would have liked it here. The river was shallow and gravelly under its shade, but it must take water from the plateau in the Wet and somewhere there would be a deep pool gouged by a fall. He saw no lancewood or any sign of old graves and did not look for them. That would be a matter for careful search if a man needed to undertake it; they would not lie near the river. But he felt them in the huge unbroken silence.

The silence brooded, heavy and aware. The dark scrub did not watch but knew it was watched; and the watcher was that high jagged line of broken rocks that made up the escarpment and the plateau. They stood shoulder to shoulder but alone, aloof from the scrub and from small living things that battled with Wet and Dry and strove to live. There were never, Wirrun thought, rocks that spoke more clearly of the age of the world, the loneliness of space or the small accident of life. They were the scarred and broken planet Earth journeying through the sky; what was carried with them they only watched.

He felt this aloof proud watching in the days that followed. Circling about his camp to look for old burial grounds, sitting at night without fire and alert for the brush of wings or the glow of red eyes, he would feel the watchful brooding and grow tense with his hand on the power. It was always the watching rocks; nothing else troubled him though he invited trouble.

Sometimes, holding the power, he sternly called for Wulgaru. Nothing answered. The power never throbbed in his hand. He began to doubt that he had found the right country and to fear that on that other night his spirit had travelled farther than he knew; but as often as he doubted his eyes would narrow in puzzled thought and he knew the answer was not so simple.

For one thing, he knew now where the country of the Yunggamurra lay and it was not far; on the night of his hunting his spirit had travelled only from here to there across the plateau. Perhaps when he fled from the waterfall he had gone out of his way, but he had come easily back to his camp. More important: even if he had missed the country of Wulgaru and the evil was not here, that did not explain the emptiness of the country.

Not only did he fail to find this Wulgaru: he found nothing. It was not natural. He could not believe that nothing lived in the river, that nothing of the Mimi type came into the rocks, that no small powerful wrestlers hid under them. There should have been times when some curious earth-thing came near, some little sly spirit of the place, and made the power throb in his hand. He could only think that they kept away, or were kept away, for some reason that he could not understand; and out of the very emptiness of the country came a puzzled conviction that was a sort of hope. He thought he had found the country of Wulgaru sure enough, and that he was being avoided.

To test it he risked his naked spirit again and hunted the mask-face in sleep. For three nights he sought it in a wide circle: hanging above the plateau, floating in tree-tops, slipping low over the grass, testing the moonlight and the dark towards morning after the moon had set. He found the lancewood scrub again and saw among its branches the rough platforms where dead men had been laid; but even here nothing moved. Wherever he went the stone-curlew cried and the night lay still. Except once: for a moment that shook him more than Wulgaru could have done and sent him back in panic flight to his trembling body. For on that night, caught between terror and longing, he glimpsed the one spirit he must not see—the water-girl.

His spirit, questing for earth-things and powers of any sort, felt at first a tingling in the air and then a throb in the shadow-shape of the stone. He went questing on down a hilltop slope of grass and under trees taller than those of the plains. In a little while he heard singing—the downward-drifting notes, the voice haunting and sharply sweet—and he wanted to call to her and knew he should go and could not do either. His spirit quivered like flame and was drawn on by the singing.

He caught words about the tall grass shining by moonlight and the land that was old by day and young by night; and he glimpsed her high in a tree and shining gold as the moon with the breeze wrapping her long dark hair about her. The song broke—she slid down from the tree and vanished and Wirrun fled too. They had found their ways out of the net and must not be caught again.

He lay in his body and trembled because she was near and had fled and because he had gone too close and could not go closer. He thought wonderingly, "Gold . . ." and forced his mind away and talked aloud, putting roughly into words a set of questions about the evil of Wulgaru. He brought the questions back to the surface of his mind and buried under them the comfort of her nearness and her singing; and a new idea of the river that flowed by his camp.

In the morning he recited his questions again and, having put them into words, rolled up his pack and made ready to leave for a time. Some of the questions had followed him across the land and still he could not answer them; he needed a man of the country. He was going back to that highway along which all men of these parts travelled, and if the People he met were not of the right country he would send a message to Derby.

The way from his first to his second camp had become familiar. He knew the shady stretches and what point to aim for by midday; it left his mind free for the questions he could not answer. Why was he being avoided? It could not be that this Wulgaru—this worst of evils, made by men and using its knowledge of them to enslave them—was afraid of a man with a power. Since it was made by a man it could not be among the First Things or the great dreamings; yet it had lived and ruled since the land was young and must have faced many men like Wirrun. He could not believe that it feared him, for that would surely make nonsense of Ko-in's tale and of Wirrun's mission.

And yet . . . it tied in with Wirrun's own feelings of doubt, of uncertainty and dissatisfaction. For this was what he had always felt—what he had tried to tell Tom Hunter, why he had journeyed west in search of Noatch—that the mask-face, though it chilled and angered him with its knowing evil, was somehow not enough. To anger and disgust the spirit-world, to justify Ko-in's tale and Wirrun's journey, there surely had to be more. Something was missing.

He remembered that he had seen this thing three times and had thought it not a terror of men but an evil. Once it had struck at him with a snake; twice he had ordered it off and it had obeyed. Only when he met it in the spirit, and it a hunter of spirits, had it seemed to defy him—and even then he had seized and made off with it and had escaped. And now, in its own country, it avoided him. To make this thing a ruler of men there had to be more to it. Something was missing.

He reached the camp by the highway while the sun was still above the horizon and made use of it to set up his camp for a day or so. He built up a useful woodheap, dug yams and fished for both dinner and breakfast. By dusk he was ready for an early vigil next day, and lit his fire and set stones to heat for grilling fish. He was breaking more wood when a pair of headlights came sweeping on to the bridge spotlighting the white railing; they faltered on the bridge, came on slowly, then turned aside and stopped.

Wirrun hunched his shoulders and muttered: some fire-ban must have been imposed and this warden or policeman was investigating. He was determined not to eat raw fish for lack of a fire and kept his head down as the fence-wires twanged and footsteps approached.

"Want a lift?" said a familiar voice at his shoulder.

Wirrun swung round incredulous and stared from under lowered brows at the firelit pock-marked face of Derby.

"Saw your fire," said Derby. "Just wondered." His jaw was tightened in the way that meant he was grinning.

"Me too," said Wirrun. "You got a job driving up and down this bit of road?"

"Yep," said Derby. "Job watching out for you."

"Yeah? And who pays you for that?"

"No money in it. Worse luck. Tommy Hunter sent word. Every man and his dog's gotta use this road. I was to watch out and help when I could. Hang on till I fetch my gear."

He strode off into the dusk, and Wirrun pushed yams into the coals of his fire and set his whole catch of fish to grill. The van's lights reached for him as it turned off the road-way to park. Derby came back with his roll swinging from one hand and his battered cooler in the other. He glanced dubiously at the fish and opened the cooler.

"Brought a bit of tucker. Seeing you're a long way from a store."

"Fine," said Wirrun, "but this time you eat with me. Food of the country. Good while since you ate that."

"Good tucker as long as there's enough. Everyone eats fish."

"There's plenty," said Wirrun with an inward grin. He felt he owed Derby something for keeping his own council in so tight-lipped a style and mentally checked the supplies in his pack. Four grilled lizard-tails to add to the fish; for afters a few young pandanus-nuts and a handful of dry woody wild apples which were nothing like apples except perhaps as to their worms.

"Where you heading?" said Derby.

"Here. Looking for you."

"So where to?"

"Back again, now I've seen you," said Wirrun taking his revenge. "That's if you know the country. I want to talk to a man of the country. So you can stuff that ignition-key you know where and lubricate your jaw for talking."

"About what?"

"If you heard from Tommy Hunter you oughta know. About this . . . Big-Cap of yours, mostly." In courtesy to Derby he would not speak the name of Wulgaru into the dark.

"Ah," said Derby. "I'll get a bit more wood."

"There's a fair heap under that old bloodwood. Use that." Wirrun reached into the cooler for plates.

Derby set to work to lay a second fire.

3

Wirrun, serving his dinner of fish and yam and lizard-tails, was glad of the cool of night but knew that in any case a second fire could not have been helped. The powers of another country, or the small earth-things of the place, may be talked of at night by one fire; for a Big-Cap like Wulgaru, and in its own country, it is wiser to talk between two. He made no comment but handed Derby his plate and set the billy to boil. Neither did Derby blench at the lizard-tails but reached for the salt and ate with calm enjoyment.

"I'll let you off the fruit course," said Wirrun kindly. "And there's still a bit of sugar left for your tea."

Afterwards he cleaned up and put away while Derby lit his second small fire and brought more wood to have at hand. They sat with their mugs of tea between the fires and blew and sipped.

"What you wanta know?" said Derby.

Wirrun was silent for a while. Derby was a good man, he thought; but so were Tom Hunter and the men of the Centre, men who had accepted him once as a hero and as a comrade too. He had had to tell those men too much and he had lost them. He did not want to lose any more good men to fear or because he had gone too far ahead of them. He wondered for a second if this was what life had made of him now—a lonely man isolated by fear; lost to his friends by being too far ahead, lost to his love by being too far behind. He turned away quickly from the thought and chose his words.

He said carefully, "They're dodging me, keeping out of

my way. All of 'em. There ought to be others besides this—thing of yours. There's nothing, all empty. I can't come to grips."

Derby frowned at the fire. "If you can't I don't see me doing better."

"But I want to know why, man—I want to know what he's up to."

"You need better than me," said Derby. "The others—the small rubbish—they'd be doing what they're told, wouldn't they? But what *he's* doing—" He shook his head. "Only—" He glanced sideways. Wirrun waited. "Only," said Derby uncertainly, "it looks good, don't it? If he's dodging? Must be he can't trust himself."

And Derby was a man of the country, one who sat between two fires to talk about Wulgaru in the dark.

"I heard he was a terror," said Wirrun.

"He's that."

"But you're telling me that in all the time he's had, all the time there is, he's never been faced before? Never met a man like me and can't handle it? Is that what you're saying?"

Derby tossed a stick on the nearer fire. "Maybe there never was a man like you. Don't know, do we? Maybe it's because you're a stranger. Not one of his own."

"Hum," said Wirrun. "Only it's been over east lately—you know that?"

"Not to say know. Heard something."

"Cheeky as a snake, not acting scared of strangers. That's why I'm here. It's your Big Cap and no one else can take it from you, but they're not having it over east."

"That's it, then," said Derby. "Why he's dodging. Hasn't got himself in charge over there yet. When he has he can handle you. That'll be it."

"Hum," said Wirrun again. He remembered that in the east the mask-face had obeyed his power but that here in its own country it had first hunted and then avoided him. "How big is this thing, then?"

Derby leaned over to make up one of the fires. "Big enough. There's those say he's only bad for bad men and for good ones he's good. Good or bad he's got 'em in his fist."

Wirrun frowned. Here was this judging of good and bad again: how could it be allowed to Wulgaru? As far as he knew there was no such judgement. There was only the law: safety or disaster for all. And men who broke it, who risked disaster for all, were punished in life by other men. He thought of those greatest powers who gave the law, whose names were spoken in secret by those who had the right. They had sometimes punished men on earth, but even they did not sit in judgement on the dead: was Wulgaru greater than these? He asked the question aloud. "Is he a Big Sunday?"

Derby shifted restlessly. "Different kettle of fish, isn't it? He made nothing. Only Clever Men; he makes them sometimes."

Wirrun nodded for he had been sure of it. They would never have sent him against one of the secret, sacred beings of the country. "So who put you in his fist? Where does he get his power over a man's spirit?"

"Where does he get it? He's got it, that's all. He takes it. There's others do the same."

"Man," said Wirrun impatiently, "I know about them. I been and looked at one on purpose. And if there's anything the same as this I don't know it yet. These others, they're hunters, that's all. Like a chicken-hawk. They might get hold of you or they might miss, depends how quick you are and if you do the proper things. But this of yours—there's no proper thing you can do. It don't hunt, it takes—and it takes the right to say if you can go home! Who gives it that right? Do all the old ones, the dreaming ones, give in to it over right and wrong? Because if they do it's the biggest of all and a sight too big for me."

Derby sat frowning at the fire, following Wirrun's argument. Wirrun waited tensely; this question, he knew, was one key to his helpless uncertainty. At last Derby turned to him, puzzled but doing his best, and picked up one phrase of the argument.

"If you can go home: he don't say that. That's out of his hands."

Wirrun breathed heavily. "All right, then, what does he say? What does he judge you for?"

"To get born again, of course. They all will, only some he'll hang on to for a good long time and clean up a bit first."

"Glory be," said Wirrun blankly. He must have been only half-awake sure enough. He had forgotten that every one of the People had at least two spirits and some of them three; that one of these was a man's own self and found its way to his right home; and that just as his body dissolved into earth and lived again in other forms so a second spirit stayed on earth to be born and live again. He had confused these two, the inviolate self and the earth-self; he had seen this Wulgaru as a man-made barrier standing between men and their dreaming. Instead it was only, like so many others, a tormenting hazard of his earthly life. No wonder Derby watched him in frowning surprise.

"Well," he said, "that cuts him down to size. I got hold of the wrong end talking to Tom—I needed a man of the country. Only . . ." He paused again and Derby waited. He had to wait some time; long enough to feed the fires again.

At last Wirrun spoke as if he were carrying on an old argument. "Look. I've seen this thing. Three times."

Derby gave his sidelong look. "You oughta be three times dead."

"I got protection," said Wirrun with a hand on his belt. "But maybe you're right, and that's what ties me up. I don't reckon this thing's big enough for all the fuss. Nasty, I'll give you that. But no bigger than others I've seen and as big as some. I don't reckon it's worth all I've heard."

"I don't reckon you've seen him then," said Derby solidly, and Wirrun was startled. "What've you seen?"

"What I was sent after," Wirrun declared; and he gave Derby a short account of the fate of Jimmy Ginger, of his own meetings with the no-thing, what he could remember of Ko-in's account, and the time he was hunted in the lance-wood scrub. Derby listened, brooding over the fire, but at the end he shook his head.

"Not him. Not his own self."

"You telling me that Ko-in and his sort wouldn't know?" Derby shook his head again. "Same thing really. These faces, they'll mean the same. Little bits of him that he's sent out; the ones he made, that he uses. But it's not like seeing the Big Boss his own self."

"Glory be," said Wirrun again. It was another thing he might have worked out for himself if his mind had ever been properly on this job. "I shoulda talked to you a long time ago."

Derby grunted in a satisfied way and after a moment ventured a comment of his own. "I been thinking. No wonder they're dodging you, man. That last time with the wings, that would've shook 'em up. You handled that right."

"Eh?" said Wirrun. "I was a fool, man. Not thinking right. Still don't know how I got out of it so easy."

"I reckon you do," said Derby. "That's the way with this lot—take a tough line and act hard. That's the only thing ever works."

"Is that right?" said Wirrun dubiously and had a sudden feeling that it was. He would never want to do it again, but in some way he did not yet understand it was as well to have looked through the kindled eyes of the mask—to have seen the dead drifting disconsolate, the land wearing away and full of fearful things, the small harmless spirits fleeing.

"You want any help?" said Derby. "There's others standing by."

"Tell 'em thanks but they sent me the right man. I see my way now. I'll be getting back early and—drag this thing out somehow. I just gotta think of something."

"Hit the sack, then," Derby suggested, "and think on your

feet tomorrer. You'll take the tucker I brought, it was got for you."

"Glad to—but no more worries, tell 'em. I been taught by experts, I don't starve in the bush."

Derby's jaw tightened again. "I seen that. Only bush tucker needs time. You might be short of it. Get off, now."

Wirrun yawned, nodded goodnight and made for his sleeping-bag. He felt released, his mind clear, and knew that he would sleep. He drifted off while he looked at Derby, still sitting hunched between the fires.

He woke in the dark between moonset and dawn, and rolled his pack and stowed away the bagful of provisions he found near it. Derby was heavily asleep, rolled in his blanket between the fires that were dead but not yet cold. Wirrun did not disturb him but only groped into the cooler to make sure that it still held something for his breakfast. Wirrun himself would breakfast by daylight somewhere up the river. He went quietly away.

It was slow walking in the dark but he had not started early for the sake of a quick journey. He had wanted to be away and alone, to be moving in the right direction and thinking as he went. When the sun rose he took time over breakfast and washed in a pool. He sat out the heat of the day beside another. There was little to be gained by reaching camp before dark.

He did reach it before sunset, and stripped and cooled off in the river again. By then he knew the source of that hard anger he had always felt against this Wulgaru: that with all the arrogance of its maker, and with no other power than evil magic and the helpless fear of men, it dared to take to itself this right of judgement. And he knew what tough, hard line he was going to take with the thing, by what means he would try to force the thing to face him. Now that he knew its limits he did not care why it avoided him—whether for Derby's reason or some other of its own. While it did avoid him he could do nothing; it must be made to face him. If it would not come to him he must go to it.

He knew only one place that the thing might call its own: the lancewood scrub. There would be others—the burial cave if he could find it, and if he must find it he would. But the lancewood scrub with its burial platforms he already knew, and that place too Wulgaru must claim as its own. Wirrun had found it empty like the rest of the country; he had been avoided there too. But if he occupied it, made it his own, stayed in it night after night, then one of two things must happen. Either Wulgaru, avoiding him, must lose this ground and accept defeat by a man or it must face the man and claim the ground.

He thought it would face him in time. A man-made thing, taking its power over man from man himself, could not afford the defeat; it would be known throughout the land and in Wulgaru's own country. It must face him.

He thought of moving his camp into the scrub and gave up the idea. In his camp a man has to sleep. He did not know his enemy and would keep his attack direct and simple; he would sleep and eat here as he had before and in the safer hours of daylight. The nights he would spend awake in the scrub. At sunset he dressed, made a small fire, ate and drank, tidied the camp and put out the fire. When the line of the escarpment was sharp against the green-glowing sky and the moon low in the east he went out of camp north to the lancewood scrub.

He went carefully with a hand on the power but it gave no sign. The stone-curlew cried and the powers of the country drew away as always. The last daylight drained from the sky as he neared the escarpment; he felt its heavy brooding and nothing else. He reached the lancewood scrub and went into its moon-patched darkness. There was nothing; it rejected him. Yet the place itself weighed on him for he was a man of the People; and he remembered the wailing spirits he had seen in it. He was glad of the small torch in his pocket, brought for the deeper darkness of the scrub.

He flashed the torch only once or twice as he found his way in, stopping often to look up into sparse leaves black against the sky. Soon he found what he was looking for: a heavier shape among the leaves, a platform where some dead man had been laid till his bones were ready for the cave. He sat down under that tree for the rest of the night.

In such a place he had no need to fight off sleep; he was tense and aware. He unwound a length of cord from the power and let it lie loose on his knee, kept a hand on the stone to receive any warning, and made himself sit relaxed like a man at rest. Now and then as the hours went by and the moon passed over he stood up and moved about a little and sat down again. Nothing else marked the hours; he expected nothing. It would take more than one night to stir Wulgaru.

At dawn he went quickly back to camp and washed and ate and slept. He woke in the afternoon, attended to firewood and water, cooked his evening meal and set out at the same time as before. This time he carried a blanket and water, both for comfort and the appearance of it.

He went to the same tree, sat there as before, and the night passed just as the first had done. By the third night, with the moon beginning to wane, he was growing accustomed to the lancewood scrub and sometimes even dozing for a moment.

On the fourth night he was jerked out of a doze by the stone throbbing in his hand.

4

If the throbbing of the stone jerked him suddenly awake at least he woke alert; he made himself limp again at once and felt for the cord that lay loose on his knee. From under his eyelids he searched the scrub, turning his head with a restless sleepy grunt. He could find no red-glowing eyes but the stone throbbed more strongly and his muscles secretly tensed.

At last he saw, on a branch just above him and much nearer than he had expected, a shadow too dark and too regular in shape. It was so near his head that he sprang in reaction even while he shouted, "Stop! I order you!" He had grabbed at the shadow and looped his cord about it before the words were out.

There was a wild wing-beating struggle like the struggle of a giant moth and the feel of something like thin dried leather. He looped it with more cord, pulled it tight and jerked his hands away. Then he pulled the torch from his pocket and flicked it on.

Small red eyes glared at him between dark enwrapping wings. The thing lay on the ground at his feet; it stirred and stilled as the light caught it. There was a wizened skull-like face between the leather wings.

"You belong to this Wulgaru?" said Wirrun.

It hissed at him.

"Did belong, more like," said Wirrun. "That's my power holding you now."

The winged thing jerked a little inside the loops of cord and was still again.

"I could keep you now, if I had any use for a thing like you." It hissed at him again. "But I haven't so I reckon I'll send you back to Wulgaru. This time, any rate. But you tell this Wulgaru not to send any more things like you against me or they mightn't be so lucky. I came here to have a few words with him but I find he's moved out. So I'm moving in. You tell him if he wants to talk about that he better come and face me under these grave-trees; himself, tell him. He needn't send any more big-eyes or bat-wings. But he better come soon, you tell him, before word gets out that I've taken over his grave-trees."

He did not order the creature with his power for he knew it would carry all it heard and saw back to Wulgaru; it had been sent for that. He began to toss free the loops of cord and wind them in; the creature jerked against the cord and lay still. When the last loop fell away it beat its wings furiously, seemed to struggle from the ground into the tree above, rustled for a moment among the leaves, then reached with its wings for the darkness and swept away. Wirrun smiled grimly and sat down to wait out the rest of the night. But he did not doze again.

For another two nights he sat under the grave-trees and felt their desolation and the country's withdrawal. The stone-curlew cried ahead of him as he came and went. He told himself that such a Big Cap as Wulgaru would not easily accept a challenge from a man; it needed time. He thought a great deal about the meeting that must come and how a man could take a tough line with Wulgaru itself—but until he knew what it was that he had to meet the thinking was wasted. Sometimes for comfort he thought of the river near his camp and that deep-laid feeling that it flowed from the water-girl to him. So near to the plateau it must, he thought, receive water from those heights; at least in the Wet and for some time after. Yet in all his wanderings in this country he had not heard a waterfall or seen a wet face of rock. Underground, perhaps . . . some fault in one of those giant gorges . . . she had seemed to vanish into the ground. It was a refuge she would know and understand.

Alone under the grave-trees night after night, with some great trial ahead that could not yet be seen, his mind gave up the memory he had buried. Gold . . . she had surely been gold . . . as when she first came through the smoke. But if some other man had caught and turned her the old Yunggamurra laws would be working again; her sisters would know where she was and would come for her. In all the time she had crawled through caverns, lost under the land, they had left her alone; only when he found and turned her had they come to take her home. Alone, then . . . an escaped Yunggamurra alone and turned to gold . . . a freed Yunggamurra? Freed by whom and from what?

On the third night after his capture of the winged creature he was so lost in these thoughts that he did not feel the faint throbbing of the stone. It was pulsing strongly before he was roused to that or the heavy chill that pressed him down. Then he tried to spring up but the cold wrapped him as his cord had wrapped Wulgaru's creature; he could make no move except to tighten his hand on the stone. And wings were beating in the trees.

He saw red eyes like firesticks in the dark, a great number of glowing eyes crowding close as the wings swept near. He could not speak to order them away. Voices hissed at him: they were close at hand.

"Dead man. Can't move, can't speak. All men dead here. This man can't speak, can't know, this dead man. This man got empty ears."

He thought he was truly dead and knew nothing of himself, but his fingers were closed on the stone. And suddenly a great tall shape stood among the others but not near or distinct; he saw it as a faint green glow, like a toadstool that glows in the dark or the glow that lights and fades in a dark moving sea. This shape spoke, and its voice came down like the sound of wind in a tall tree.

"Who waits for Wulgaru under the grave-trees? Say what man you are."

And he thought he was no man; that he was dead and had no answer. The leather wings swooped by his face, the fiery eyes shone close, and behind them the tall shape glowed green.

"Say what you are," it called again.

And suddenly in Wirrun's mind another great voice spoke with passion: *Poor spirit, will you not speak for it? Will you not say what the stars will stoop to hear?* And he opened his dead lips and answered.

"I am." Again he could say no more—yet as he said this he knew himself. "I am!" he cried more strongly. The wings faltered and the fiery eyes flickered; the green glow pulsed. But Wulgaru spoke again like a tree and ordered him.

"Say who you are."

"You know that," said Wirrun grimly through the crushing cold that still held him down. "Ask who I'm from."

The shape of Wulgaru laughed a great sneering laugh. "I know that too! From shadows and nothings, things that creep like beetles out of the land and are bound by its law."

"And that's the law they send you. It's too big for you, mate."

The shape laughed again. "A law of beaten sand and crumbled rock and dust carried on the wind, a law of lost water and dead seas. What is that to me? I take my law from the living and knowing, from Man—I take it and make it my own. What is the land to me?"

Then Wirrun was angry for he had looked through the eyes of the mask and seen for himself the lies of Wulgaru. His anger melted the cold and he sprang up at last and faced the green-lit shape. It dimmed and gathered itself again; the red-glowing eyes hung near it and the wings rustled among leaves.

"Big words for a thing that a man made out of a tree!" shouted Wirrun. "I'll tell you what the land is to you—

outside this country it throws you off like an old dead dog! Here you belong to the men that made you, and as long as they give it to you this is your place. Stick to it. I'm ordering you. Where I come from men don't give up their law to a man-made thing like you."

"Do they not?" The voice was softly mocking. "Then Wulgaru has lost his ears and must hide in a cave among bones. I dreamed that where you come from men give up their law for man-made things far smaller than Wulgaru. Do they not give their children man-made toys instead of love? And kill themselves every day in man-made fun? And give away their law for man-made power and man-made empty hate? I thought I saw this. Poor Wulgaru: he dreamed that in the east men threw away their law and begged for him."

"And who did you dream gave you the right to say so, you bit of tree?" The shape shone green with anger and Wirrun clutched his stone. It took all his strength to speak so boldly, but his mind tightened like his fingers and clutched at what he knew: that Wulgaru had avoided him and that only boldness would do.

And Wulgaru answered calmly, even kindly. "Man gives me the right for who else could? What else is there?"

"Not me," said Wirrun. "I give you nothing. So if that's your right there's a hole in it."

"It is a hole I must bear, for who would seek rights over Wirrun of the People, Ice-Fighter, Peace-Bringer, a man born Clever? His greatness sets him apart from men."

And is that all your greatness? An axe falls on it . . .

"You're selling me short," Wirrun retorted. "It's not on account of the big names that I throw you off. I just spit on you because I am."

At that the anger of Wulgaru broke through. "A little reason! Because you are. Because the winds blow this way or that, the flower falls or fruits, the cicada sings or dies in the shell. Only for that?"

"For all of that."

"Only for that you stand under my grave-tree and order me? You have strange dreams, little stranger."

"No stranger," said Wirrun shortly, holding hard to his strength. "If I never stood here before I stand here by right. I've been given all the land for my country. And I see you don't turn me out. Took your time to face me, didn't you?"

"I don't face you now," said Wulgaru sharply. "If I faced you, Little Am, you would not speak so loud. You would be a skin-and-bone fellow, one of the poor sort that wail about you now if I could show them to you."

"I've seen 'em."

The green glow dimmed and gathered itself again. "It is my kindness to the hero Ice-Fighter that I do not face you."

"And is that what I'm to go back and tell 'em? That Wulgaru's a terror for dead men but he was too kind to face one live man? There'll be one big laugh all over the land. Every tree and rock and swamp and claypan'll be laughing at the kindness of Wulgaru. Any rate I won't be going back for a bit, I reckon. I like it here. I'll just be camping in this bit of scrub till your kindness runs out and you ask for your grave-trees back. And then, if you promise to keep yourself and your brood at home, maybe I'll let you have 'em."

He quailed inside and clutched the stone for Wulgaru roared his answer like a storm-wind among trees. "Face you, you half-made thing—face you! But will you dare face me? You talk-talk-talk like a cockatoo and hide away inside your flesh but will you come out of it and face me? Will you face me truly, in your spirit, eh? Or will they laugh at *you* across the land?"

Trembling as he was, Wirrun forced his voice to be strong. "I'll face you any way you like. Say how and when."

"Ah!" breathed the shape; and yet it was silent for a while. When it spoke again there was neither anger nor triumph in the tree-tall voice but a tone almost of sadness, like the west wind among she-oaks. "You have claimed this country as yours, you shall face me like a man of the country.

When night comes again you shall sleep at your own fire with the bag you wear, and the power within, to guard your sleeping flesh. But your spirit shall lie unguarded up there in the branches where other men have lain; and you shall be brought to face me truly, and I will destroy you."

He did not know how he could meet this test but only that he could not avoid it—and that he would not be parted from the stone for he did not go into battle in order to lose. He said, "It's me you're supposed to be facing and not some other man. Where I go the stone goes: its outside with mine and its spirit with mine. But I'll give my word not to use it against you. If you destroy me that's that, I can't do more. But if you don't you stay in your own place ever after, you and all your sort. Give me your word for that or it's off and I'll carry on the way I am." He waited grimly and when no answer came shouted, "Come on, Wulgaru. A Big Cap like you, you can't be scared of a bit of quartz on one man's belt."

It answered sombrely. "You speak what you do not know, you and your little stone. If I do not defeat you still I must destroy you; you cannot face me unchanged. But I will take your words as you meant them: if I do not destroy you like another man I and mine will keep to our place for always. It is agreed."

For a moment the scrub was hung with glowing eyes and beaten by the sweep of wings. Then it was still, the cold drained out of it and the shapes all gone; there was only the heavy silence of the grave-trees, dark branches and thin leaves against the sky, and the darker shape of the platform of the dead on which Wirrun must lie.

5

Wirrun went out from the grave-trees and sat unsleeping under the stars. They were paled by the pale gold of moonlight but the edge of the scrub hid the moon. At first Wirrun was weak and shaking, for to face even the veiled shadow of Wulgaru had cost all his strength. Later he was heavily weary but far from sleep. His mind shrank from the test to come and could find no way to withstand it; it seemed that some force beyond himself or Wulgaru, some tide as deep and quiet as the moonlight, had lifted him and brought him to this night.

He remembered Jimmy Ginger washing in his net, and the snake that was set in his way, and how against all reason his defiant spirit had seized the mask, and the old and bitter view he had seen through its eyes. That had been Wulgaru's view; he had seen with Wulgaru's own eyes; he sat with his brow drawn heavily down and tried to turn that view on himself and the struggle. He could see nothing clear. He felt only that deeper tide sweeping them on and a sense of loss and of power turned knowingly against itself. He did not know what that meant, unless it were aimed at his stone.

He thought of Noatch, thief of souls and hungry for warmth, trapped in a red box lined with mirrors; and he knew that he could invent no trap for the wise and knowing evil of Wulgaru. He thought of his body left empty and asleep in the country of the enemy, and he shivered again. That was the danger to be dreaded. His spirit would be alive and aware and could meet what came according to its strength; but if they destroyed his senseless body while he was away he would have no earthly escape. That must be guarded against; he thought the threat or warning of it lay in the last words of Wulgaru.

At daylight he rose and turned back to his camp and nothing peeped at him as he went. There was only the old land stirring, setting itself against the sun for one more day. He thought that if he must be destroyed he would choose to have it here, under the aloof and watching rocks. He found himself looking on at his own life as men are supposed to do in drowning: none of it easy, much of it hard and bitter, but all of it enriching. He would not give it up easily.

He could never choose Ularra's way—that had been a lie told by angry self-pity. He could choose only life and more of it, lived more freely. More of day and night and rocks and tall, remembered trees, of singing recaptured and dark hair seen again; of wind-riding and friendship and fear. It was good to be sure of it before he met Wulgaru. He was thinking this when he came in sight of his camp and saw smoke rising from his fireplace.

He told himself he should be wary but there was that sense of being lifted and carried on to some unavoidable end. He knew who had lit his fire and sent the smell of bacon wafting towards the escarpment; and when he reached the camp it was indeed Derby's scarred face that looked up from the frying-pan. It was like the chime of a bell to see him there.

"Still spying on me," said Wirrun, his voice ragged from weariness.

"Few stores in case you're running low," said Derby. "See you got those bleeding eyes again. Breakfast's ready."

Wirrun sat down and accepted bacon and eggs. "You been walking all night?"

"Yesterday," Derby explained. "Smelt your fire and got in just on dark. You were out."

They shared bacon and eggs in silence and Wirrun savoured the luxury of the sharing. When they both sat with their mugs of hot tea he said, "Planning to leave right away, are you?" and grinned to see Derby frowning at the fire.

"Thought I'd give it a day or two," said Derby at last. "Man of the country. Might be some good."

"Too good a man to waste," said Wirrun. "This is no place for a man of the country. You're leaving right away."

"What's on then?" said Derby postponing argument, and Wirrun gave him the barest outline of the night past and the one to come. Derby wasted no time on the unforeseeable but went straight to the point that could be foreseen.

"It's not a thing a man can do," he said roundly. "The rest can come at you asleep while you're off busy with the Boss one."

"It's not a thing I can leave," said Wirrun.

"You need someone standing by. I know the business, what there is."

"Sure you do but I'm not trusting it. I got safer plans. No knowing how long this sleep-journey might take, and a man on guard'd have to sleep himself sooner or later. I'm not risking it any rate—I want to see you round again and not be tied up worrying. If a man of the country was wanted he'd have been sent, but they sent me. You finish your tea and take your pack and get off down that river."

"Not me," said Derby solidly and they drank in silence a while longer.

"Man," said Wirrun at last, "you've been more good than you know—what I needed most you've just given it to me. But I reckon I know where to go for help. Now you do what's gotta be done, same as me."

Derby frowned again but found nothing else to say. He said nothing till the camp was cleared up and he stood with his pack on his shoulder ready to leave. Then he said, "Make a smoke if you need me. And for god's sake get some sleep."

"I'll do that," said Wirrun, "and thanks, mate."

He watched Derby slouch away down the river; whatever might happen, there went a man who would know a bit about it. Enough for word to pass. When he had gone Wirrun himself took a last look at the fire for safety and, leaving his pack where it lay, turned away up the river.

It was hard to find from the ground, by daylight and with only his eyes, what he had seen once by moonlight as he floated above. But he thought the upper course of the river might set him on his way, and with the escarpment so near he should soon know. The heat was beginning to swell but the flood-scoured banks of the river, hung with paperbark and ghost gum, made their own shade. He kept to the reaches of sand and gravel in the river-bed; almost at once it became a series of wide shallow pools and flowed partly under its bars of gravel and sand.

Between paper-wrapped trunks and under screens of drooping leaves the mosquitoes hummed. The river-bed was narrowed by rocks, widened and was narrowed again. He reached the outlying hills near the escarpment and still there was no whisper of falling water. A deep pool ahead was partly hidden by two twisted leaning gums; he pushed through the leaves and saw beyond them a hillside. There was no more river.

It had gone underground.

The broken rocks edging the farther end of the pool were not damp but wet, and above them rose the hill. Now that his eyes saw it he knew that his spirit had seen it before. He filled his water-bag, rested for a moment, and went out into the heat and began to climb.

It was a tough steep climb up the broken hillside. It was hard to believe that above there could be tall trees and slopes of brown grass. But when he came between high rocks on to the hilltop he saw that it sloped gently away to grass and distant trees; some trick of winds or circle of harder rock had built up a sandy soil here instead of tearing it away. He went on down the slope.

An ocean of silence flooded the world and drowned the plains below; small sounds of birds and insects floated in it for a moment and washed away. Wirrun thought he heard a song dropping into it note by note; he wandered on from shade to shade with his hand on the power, hearing but not hearing the sweet clear notes and sometimes murmuring as he walked.

"You know it's me, girl, but don't be scared . . . It's all over, can't be helped, you said we couldn't win . . . I wouldn't take away what you've got, I just need a bit of help. If you don't like it you just say . . . Only I can trust you, see, a man can count on you . . . Let me come, water-girl, just the once . . ."

He drifted on murmuring to the enormous silence, seeing trees that his eyes had never seen before and unable to choose between them. But the power tingled a little in his hand and the notes he could not hear trembled in the silence and he knew she was near.

Then the power began to throb, and looking quietly about he saw that after all he was watched and heard. A figure went with him from shade to shade watching secretly behind tree-trunks and rocks, rustling after him in the long grass. He could never fully see it except that it was bent and awkward, and that sometimes a sharp awn of grass moved and became a long sharp nose; and at first he wondered if some evil jailer had shut the water-girl away. But his spirit rejected that idea with conviction, and his memory of her singing by moonlight denied it too.

At last he found himself returning again and again to one tree and stood and looked at it. She had vanished into the ground . . . to the underground stream . . . There seemed to be no opening a man could see, and if there were he could not enter. He must wait till she came. This place was hers, it was her peace and safety; he could not go in unasked.

And suddenly that bent and awkward figure stood at the base of the tree and he saw it fully. It stood half crouched, wearing a broad belt of hair, and looked at him earnestly with eyes squinted against the light, its long nose as sharp as any grass-awn. And in its watching squinted eyes he saw the watching remoteness of the rocks and the immensity of the silence and the old patient endurance of the land; but he saw them caring, and he went without question to the spot to which the figure pointed and found a pothole and climbed through.

He fell on to sand and into dark coolness. He could see nothing yet, but he knew the Yunggamurra was there and spoke humbly to the dark. "Don't be scared. Don't be angry. I was going to wait but I was sent."

There was no answer.

"I'll go if you say. Any rate I won't come back. Only I wish you'd listen first."

He heard her voice a little way off: "Who sent you?"

"Bent up; sharp nose; squinty eyes; a Great One but gentle." He was beginning to see in the dimness of the cavern.

"He-of-the-Long-Grass," she murmured. "He was a dreaming once."

"You can feel it." She was crouched at the far end of the cavern, glimmering softly gold with the dark hair moving on her shoulders. She wore her only defense, that look of cool indifference that had always moved him. He spoke with a broken tenderness that he could not help.

"Water-girl. Don't worry. We couldn't help it, we had no chance. Man and spirit, it's not meant to be; I know that now. Only I needed you so bad, you're all a man can trust."

She cried, "You cannot trust me! Have I not played the Yunggamurra's game? I gave you happiness and broke it— you cannot trust the Yunggamurra!"

He smiled. "You always told me only I never listened. And the happiness was worth the breaking. But there's nothing else I want to trust like I trust you, that's something still between us. And if I'm wrong I won't complain."

She looked at him in silence for so long that at last he pleaded. "This old one, Long Grass; he's not like most. He's a looking-after sort."

"That is his beauty. Even a Yunggamurra knows it."

"He wouldn't have sent me if it wasn't right."

She said, "Tell me your need."

So he told her how Wulgaru had come east and he was sent to keep it in its place; of all that had happened in the forest and how his spirit must go out of him to meet and withstand Wulgaru. And her eyes widened in fear and were moonlit and darkened by turn, but Wirrun was too troubled and weary to notice.

"So they get two chances to my one. If the Big Boss gets hold of my spirit I'm done; but while that's going on there's the rest of me asleep and the others can have a go at that, and then I'm done anyway. It wins even if I win."

"I do not think Wulgaru means such a trick, but there are other chances. You wish to sleep safely watched?"

"If you'd do that for me, water-girl—if you'd let me sleep here and stay by till I wake—then I'd go off sure. And after I'd forget I ever saw you again."

"And if Wulgaru wins? If I stay by and never see you wake?"

He frowned. "I never thought of that . . . Would this Long Grass help? Get rid of me for you? Find you another cave?"

"Oh Man!" she cried in pain and anger.

He was cast down, troubled and still frowning. After a moment he raised his eyes and found hers watching him. They sat at opposite ends of the cavern and looked at each other while the small clear stream trickled from him to her and away into the darkness.

"Gold," he said at last. "What happened to your silver?"

She stirred restlessly. "It will grow again in the right mud . . . It was the sun. I was caught among rocks. I was too dried to use my senses."

He nodded. "Well, with gold you can have the sun and the water too. I've seen your sisters. They don't know where you've got to. You don't want to go back?"

"It is hard to be alone. But I keep my own self."

He nodded again. "And you're free."

"If I were caught again they would find me and bring me home."

He smiled. "And you'd run off again. And find another place. And keep your own self. You don't need them any more, or Wirrun-and-Murra either. You're free. And now, while I can still keep awake, I better do the same. Find another place to sleep."

"You will wait," she said, "while I bring grass. There is no other place. You will sleep here."

He could not speak. He only drew away to leave room while she climbed the rocks to the pot-hole above. In the corner where he now stood there was a blackening of the cavern wall. With a bushman's instinct he looked for and found the little heap of charred wood and ash, and stood looking at it while he waited.

Only weeks ago she had sat by his fire drawn and yet distrustful; a human girl who had not outgrown her Yunggamurra dread. But here, a Yunggamurra again and alone in her cavern, she had made her own fire.

SIX

In the Cave of Wulgaru

I

Wirrun waited with nervous irritation in the cavern. It was past midday already and his body, strained by the fearful night under the grave-trees, ached for sleep; whatever waking time was left he did not want to spend waiting alone while that golden ripple of a Yunggamurra gathered a mound of grass. This was the last chance of his life to be with her a little while, to hear her speak and look at her again. He could have gathered grass for himself—tired as he was, he could have slept on broken boulders.

While he was thinking this the light in the cavern blinked and brown-gold grass came spilling through the pot-hole into a great mound beneath. After it came the Yunggamurra, bouncing lightly into the grass with a bubble of laughter She climbed out of it still laughing; he could see her planning to turn the pot-hole entrance into a game.

"Leave it," he said shortly. "I can sleep on rock."

"He-of-the-Long-Grass sends it," she said severely. She fished in the heap for a woven-grass bag. "And these." She gave him the bag and he saw that it held flat scorched cakes of coarsely ground grass-seed.

"It's early yet," he said fretfully. "I just want to see you for a bit before I sleep."

"You see me now. Eat."

"I'm not hungry."

"That is not important. You bring me your human self to care for and I bring you the help of the Long Grass. Sit there and eat."

He sat and chewed unwillingly at the hard grass-seed

cakes and watched her body gleaming in the dimness as she carried bundles of grass into a corner for his bed. The little river slid over its rock and its water rustled softer than the grass.

"A man needs to be more than a man," he grumbled.

She tossed her head and was wrapped in hair. "And the wind blows and the sky is blue and the sun will rise tomorrow. You are weary beyond sense. You must sleep soon, for while sleep is heavy it keeps the spirit in."

She came out of the darker corner and sat watching him eat. "Weary or strong," she said, "you must listen a moment. For if the powers of this country have avoided you you cannot know them."

"I thought I did," he said grimly remembering the night.

"There are others. I do not speak of small earth-things, my own kind, but of older and stronger powers. There are those whose work is joined to the work of Wulgaru. If, as it seems, he was unwilling to face you he may call on the help of these others."

Wirrun frowned. "What others?"

"Some are called Moomba. They look like men but they draw the life from men. Wulgaru waits for the shades of the dead; these send them to him. Watch for the Moomba."

"It's supposed to be only him and me and that was bad enough. Well . . . what else?"

"There are those that guard the law. If it is broken they too may send men to Wulgaru."

He frowned again. "I'm no law-breaker."

"You know where in this country a man may walk and where is forbidden? What foods may be eaten in what season? You are free of this country as any man born here, that is known; but if Wulgaru seeks to trap you are you prepared?"

He was silent.

"Watch for Kurakun, shaped like the smoke-hawk. Its business is with marriage. Watch for the Lundji, great black dogs that nose out law-breakers and destroy them."

"I'm used to dogs any rate. Is that the lot?"

"Only one more word before you sleep. There are powers in the land that are guarded against by fire or by water, and some by the beating of weapons and loud noise; some fear a kind of stone or wood and some may be sung. Against Wulgaru there is only one guard and it is harder than the rest: it is courage. If you can meet him calmly and boldly you can save yourself. And so I have no fear for you."

Wirrun gave a twisted smile. "That's one of us any rate. I'll do my best."

"Sleep, then."

"Not yet, water-girl, there's time yet. I'll never talk to you again. Sleep can wait."

"No, it cannot. I will not sit by and see you lose because sleep held you too tight. Go to your bed, Man, while the Yunggamurra sings."

Wearily he knew she was right. His eyes turned to the scorch-marks on the rocks: hiding alone, she had made a fire in memory of him. She had taken him into her safe and secret cave, fed and advised him and promised to guard him. Now she reminded him of what they were: he man and she Yunggamurra, the cruel and beautiful and vanishing thing that a man could not have. He went at once and lay on his bed of grass.

"You better try and sing me up some of this courage," he said giving himself the last word.

"If you needed it you would not be here," she retorted taking it from him; and she sang no song of courage or power but only of the grass whispering in the wind and a tiny lizard hiding. And within a minute he slept.

The Yunggamurra sat like a lizard herself, not near but alert in her stillness. She sat while the water whispered in the cavern, while the day moved on and the sun set and the light from the pot-hole faded. With eyes that had long ago learnt to see in caverns she watched unmoving; and at last she saw the man's sleep change.

His body stirred, loosened and relaxed. A mist flowed out of it and hung for a moment and gathered itself. She saw the spirit-shape of the man Wirrun. He seemed to stand in air just above his sleeping self and to reach high up in the cavern with the shape of the power still hung at his waist; and he looked at her steadily with love and gratitude and perhaps farewell, and the Yunggamurra stood up and looked back.

They did not speak though they knew they might have done, for they were still man and earth-thing; since the barrier of his flesh was put aside they set silence between them. But she lifted her chin with the free, fierce pride of the Yunggamurra and showed him her moonlit eyes full of faith, and he smiled and bent his head and rose up out of the cavern. Then she sat on the rocks by his sleeping form and watched again and sometimes sang.

Wirrun hung in darkness under the stars for the moon would not rise for many hours. He knew the dark did not hide him but he felt hidden and was glad. Yet for safety he turned away from the lancewood scrub and circled east and north over the plateau before he turned west again. So he came over the edge of the escarpment and down into the scrub.

Nothing followed him; he was avoided still. Nothing brooded in the lancewood scrub but its own heavy stillness and waiting dark. He drifted low through trees till he found the one he knew and rose to the dark shape in its branches. The platform was made of saplings tied in place with red-ochred string. Broad sheets of papery bark lay on it. Wirrun did not fully know the proper ways of the country, but after a moment's pause he crept between the sheets of paperbark and lay covered.

The bark weighed him down as the cold had done before. There was nothing to come between him and his fear: no throbbing of blood or tightening of muscle or deep-drawn breathing. He had not known how a man's body, responding to fear, can shut him away from it. Now he was alone with fear. Shadow-hand on shadow-stone he looked for help.

No help came. He had received all that could be given

and must manage the rest for himself. But in a while he found strength. It crept into his spirit mysteriously, hidden in scraps of memory and whispered in many voices. Wind-journeys over the land that had once been young and swallowed seas . . . *Am I more than the land?* Majestic flooded gum trees in the east, white ghost gums in the Centre, twisted and stunted gums of the north . . . *See, I have caught a tree!* Dark faces authoritative with age, quiet and waiting like the great rocks . . . *You've gone too far ahead of us, son.* The great black dog flowing under him, the Pungalunga rearing out of the river, the Jannoks spinning in the willy-willy . . . *A man of power . . . you are the Man . . . Maybe there never was a man like you.* The wildness of a storm over the water, and voices singing and howling in the storm . . . *You cannot trust the Yunggamurra!* . . . *But there's nothing else I want to trust.*

From these scraps and more his spirit gathered strength. The unknown was terrible, the fear would grow, but he would meet them as boldly as he could . . . *And so I have no fear for you.* And as he gained this foothold on fear he felt the cold of Wulgaru through the heavy cover of bark, and the stone throbbing in his hand, and heard the branches rustling a little way off and knew he was looked for.

2

With the sweep and hush of wings through the trees came the rustle of leaves and the creak of branches: they were working towards him by some plan, going from one to another of the dark quiet platforms where dead men had been laid. The waiting was bad but it did not test his courage, for the bark cover and the heavy cold weighed him down and he could not move. He heard them in the next tree, in the next branch. His cover was lifted, red eyes flared and a word was spoken.

"One."

He was covered again. The grave-tree was silent.

In time a scuffling and muttering broke out below. The tree trembled and began to sway, not the branches only but the whole tree. He felt himself lifted, lying on his platform under the bark: the tree itself was rising.

He would not lie like death and face his fear unknowing. Anger stirred him to move a little; the bark slid aside and he looked into the dark. And first he looked up through branches to the stars.

They blazed white and very near: not the stars men knew in these days but those men had always known, a cold white blaze in the sky. He was carried so near that it seemed the soft black sky might drape and smother him. In a spasm of fear he turned his face aside and looked down.

The trunk of the tree reached far down out of sight. The lancewood scrub was gone. By the light of the terrible stars he saw a wide and dreary plain. It shimmered a little like the magic waters of the desert, and gathered on the plain he saw the crowd of the dead. Shoulder to shoulder they stood and covered the plain for they had been gathering a long time. They stood listless and drooping, and as the grave-tree passed over they raised hopeless faces and looked up. Their faces filled him with terror: ghost-whitened faces of the People but all now without hope or pride, for these were the dead that Wulgaru judged evil. Some wore the scars of their manhood, some wore red ochre in beard and hair, but all were lost. He saw one alone and bewildered staring up from a tangled fishing-net.

Suddenly the sky rang with a sound of clapping, regular and rhythmic, and a great voice began to chant. And on the plain the dead began to dance, shuffling and swaying to the freakish call of tap-sticks and songman. The grave-tree was gone like a dream. Wirrun stood on the plain among the dead and their weary despair wrapped him as the cold had done. They flowed past him following the tap-sticks and the song and turned their darkened eyes to him and called in empty voices that he must come. He went with them, drawn by the calling and the music, and saw great rocks darkening ahead and in them the mouth of a cave. The crowd of the dead flowed into it taking him with them.

He passed between cleft cracked walls of sandstone and saw painted on them a thousand years of dreaming: animals and men, ancestors and beings not to be named. Some were faded into ghostly shapes like the crowd that led him, some were kept bright and clear through all time. Mystery-beings in mystery-dress gazed down from huge dark eyes, but the crowd of the dead bore him under these and deeper in beyond the starlight. He saw ahead the changing light of a fire and went on with the others into a wider cavern. And at last, by the wavering light of flames, he faced Wulgaru.

It sat sprawled on a stone in the firelight. Its head and body were cut from a tree-trunk, its arms and legs from branches. Its joints were round river-stones tied with red-painted string. Its face was a clumsy mask like those he had seen before but greater and more terrible. Wirrun's hand went to his belt and he tried to draw into his being all the strength of the stone, for the thing called Wulgaru was roughly made but with a fearful power.

It sprawled on its stone as if to let him look and the timid dead drifted back against the cavern walls. Wirrun stood free of them at last. He saw perched behind Wulgaru a great grey falcon, the smoke-hawk Kurakun, and crouched at each side a monstrous black dog, the Lundji, with red leaf-shaped eyes and their red tongues lolling. But he could not look at them for Wulgaru suddenly opened its jaws and snapped them shut with a sound that rang in the cavern. Then it lifted its head and looked at him, and its eyes blazed white like the terrible stars.

"I welcome you," it said in its great voice like a windy tree, "Man of the east who mated with the Yunggamurra of the west." Behind it the smoke-hawk stirred and lifted its wings but Wirrun had no fear of the smoke-hawk.

"I've been told," he answered as boldly as he could, "that if a man mates with magic he's swallowed or he grows. Maybe you'll swallow me, Wulgaru, but you haven't done it yet. I've got time to grow."

The smoke-hawk settled and the mask of Wulgaru smiled. It spoke again as if for the first time.

"I welcome you, Man of the east; you who have come through the secret cave and seen what the law forbids."

The two great dogs sprang up, stiff-legged and snarling. The black hair bristled on their shoulders and the rattling of their snarls echoed in the cavern and grew.

"I came by the way I was brought," said Wirrun, "and I had the right. The whole land knows all countries are mine and this one too. That's why I'm sent."

But the dogs stood snarling and Wulgaru said, "There are degrees of manhood. Not all our men have the right to see that cave. Where are the marks that show your right?"

"I need no marks. I take the right from those that sent me."

Then the snarling rose and the great dogs leapt and he knew that if he were torn in pieces he must not show fear. He saw their red eyes and red mouths, and since he could not use the power and had nothing else he lunged out with an arm against the dogs and waited for the crunch of teeth.

But the dogs faltered, ears and tails flattened. Their red eyes were angry but they would not attack and at last slunk back. Wirrun tried not to show bewilderment, but he spread his fingers and stared at the hand that the dogs would not bite.

A single hair lay in it, a long coarse hair as black as the Lundji's. A hair of the Jugi. It had been entangled in possum-fur cord or rough bark twine since he rode away from Ko-in on that other great black dog—or it had come into his hand by spirit means—it did not matter. He held it out to Wulgaru.

"There's the mark of my right," he said grimly. "From those that sent me."

The white fire of Wulgaru's eyes blazed for a moment but it spoke as calmly as before.

"I welcome you, Man of the east whose living spirit comes before its time into the cave of the dead."

Then the crowd of the dead raised a howling and screeching and broke towards Wirrun in a wave from the cavern walls, all their darkened eyes staring at him and their ghost-white hands reaching to claw and tear him. They were more dreadful than the dogs but still he must be bold: he took a great leap forward and grasped the shoulder of Wulgaru and stood close between the monster and the snarling Lundji. And as the howling dead hung back he shouted to them.

"There's one of you there in a net. Let him come out."

The crowd of the dead wailed and drifted and stared with their empty eyes; but in their drifting a way opened and the ghost stood there that stared hopeless and bewildered from its tangled fishing-net. And Wirrun was filled with anger and swung round to accuse Wulgaru.

"This was a man from the east. He's got his own dreaming. If he's broke your law that's because it wasn't his. What's he doing here?"

Wulgaru's eyes blazed again. "He is mine and so he is here. What is he to you or his dreaming to me? I took him, and those I take must follow my law."

"There's a bigger one. You and all these know it: a man's got a right to his own dreaming. If he leaves it and comes here that's his risk—but this man died in his own country and there's a road waiting for him over there. You set yourself up over right and wrong, you turned your dogs on me for breaking the law. Well now I name you, Wulgaru, breaker of the law. I call on all the powers of this country to send this spirit home. And what are these Lundji dogs going to do about that?"

The cavern was filled with a wild outcry but the fire, that had burned bright though it was not fed, sank low. Wirrun only heard the angry baying of the Lundji, the beat and flurry of wings, the fearful crying of the dead; he saw only their whirling shapes and the white fire of Wulgaru's eyes. And in the midst of this fury and flurry the voice of Jimmy Ginger cried, "Home!"

The fire sprang high again. The Lundji and the smoke-hawk and all the crowd of the dead had gone and Wulgaru sat unmoved. "You have won a ghost," he said with a sneer.

"I've won something, then," said Wirrun stoutly in the face of his disappointment.

The sneer vanished and Wulgaru laughed a little. "And did you hope to win more? To see me torn in pieces, say? Must I teach you victory?"

Wirrun only gazed sternly back. He would not be fooled by any trickery of words; he was not yet a victor for his spirit was still held to Wulgaru and he knew it. Wulgaru laughed again.

"Should the law of the country be torn in pieces when the law of the land is made whole? You have finished your work, Man. For if the powers of the country take from me the ghost of the eastern dreaming how can I hold any other but my own? You have turned my country on me. It will hold me to the law for all time."

Wirrun gazed in doubt and hope into the star-white eyes of the mask. He thought that truth was in them, and something darker that filled him with dread. He waited.

"And now," said Wulgaru in its voice like the wind in trees, "since you have laid your hand on me we fight. And we shall find out who and what you are."

The cavern was filled with the echoing rhythm of tap-sticks. Though the crowd of the dead was gone Wirrun saw that other man-shapes stood against the sandstone walls. And he knew them for the Moomba who drain the life out of men.

3

Wirrun's spirit was heavy with fear for he saw that no light live spirit could win a fight with the great log-shape of Wulgaru. If courage was his only defense he had lost already, but he seized the vanishing tail of courage and made himself stand straight and look bold.

"If you destroy me," he said, "you'll send my ghost home."

"Yourself you have made it sure. But if a man claims all countries where is home?"

That was a cold question that Wirrun could not now face. "We'll find that out too," was all he said.

The monster smiled. It stood up clumsily and began to shuffle and stamp to the tapsticks, loose-jointed and grotesque. Wirrun watched grimly. It came to him that Wulgaru was showing itself man-made and clumsy to catch him off his guard. He was not fooled; he knew power when he saw it.

"Come," said Wulgaru and danced away out of the cavern. The Moomba went after it tapping to its dance and Wirrun followed.

They went through the dark passage and under the painted eyes of the outer cave and on to the plain. The terrible stars were gone and it seemed daylight. Wulgaru's stone-jointed arms swung loose and crashed the tops off trees. It snapped its jaws in time with the tapsticks and sent parrots screeching away. Now it seemed too powerful for any live thing to approach and he thought he could only try to use the lightness and speed of his spirit.

"Here," said Wulgaru at last, and the tapsticks were silent

and the Moomba stood aside. "The ground is clear and level. Does this place suit you, little Man? I would not have it said in the land that Wulgaru defeated the Ice-Fighter unfairly."

If he was being taunted he would not rise to the bait. He said only, "One place is as good as another."

Wulgaru smiled again and turned to face him. "Are you ready, then, Hero?"

"Ready as I'll ever be," said Wirrun alert and watchful.

Without any further word the thing lunged at him. He whirled aside and let it pass. It brought up with a crash against a tree that rocked and swayed.

"You will not fight?" it said politely.

"I'm not a tree," said Wirrun. "I use what I've got." He side-whirled again and reached quickly for a fallen branch. At the third pass he managed to thrust the branch between the thing's wooden legs. It fell with a crash that rattled its joints and sprang up again.

"Ah," it said, and reached out an arm as quick as light and drew him close.

Water, he thought desperately, I'm water; he made himself inert and fluid and slid down out of its grasp. But in a moment it had him again.

They fought like two spirits, both light and lightning-fast, a slippery sort of wrestling in which Wirrun held his own for a while. In a moment they fought like two strong men; they fell and sprang and grunted and struggled while dust rose about them and one reached for a stone or another a stick. That too changed in a flash and they fought like man and power; and Wirrun found himself helpless, held un-moving, weakening into nothing even while he fought to fight. And from very far away the voice of Wulgaru reached him as solemn and sad as the wind in she-oaks.

"For though I am man-made, a bit of tree, yet am I death. You cannot meet me unchanged."

Defeated, he slid away into some long winding dark.

Yet he would not submit. Darkness contained him but

from within it he knew the sun still beat down on the plain and the dust had not settled. Hands seized him and he knew they were the hands of the Moomba. Now he could see again: they slid him into a grass-woven net and hoisted it into a tree and set him swinging. And while he swung gently to and fro they sang with great sweetness.

He was weary, weary . . . he had journeyed over the land . . . hunted and been hunted, watched many nights under the grave-trees, entered the secret world of the dead and set free the captive ghosts. Victory was his . . . he had earned the right to sleep . . . he slept . . .

The darkness was real and immediate and smelled of old death. The net bound him close and he could not move. The darkness was a cave and all around, in every crack and niche and hollow of worn sandstone, were the pale skulls and bones of men. They were so still; they forced themselves on him out of the dark with their powerful, oppressive stillness.

He knew he was in that darkness beyond the painted cave, bound as other men had been and laid in the last burial-place of these People. He was laid here by the Moomba and could never escape. The heaviness of death smothered him and nothing came between him and his fear.

He could not bear this fear—he must escape it. He struggled for life, for his memories of days and night, the love of Ko-in, the trust of Ularra, the faith of the golden Yung-gamurra. And as he set these things between him and fear he saw that in the very fear itself he was still himself. He was not yet nothing. He knew himself.

"I am," he whispered stiffly.

The heaviness of death lifted a little.

"I am."

The air moved and sweetened as if a breeze had stirred it.

"I am . . . I am . . ."

The bones of the dead were pitiful: neat puppets made for children, broken and untidy now.

"The bit of me here, it's spirit. They can't make bones out of that."

He found that he could move a little, enough to loosen the net. It opened easily. He slid free.

At that same moment in another cave, in her own cavern where the river ran, the Yunggamurra stirred and stilled. There was a change. She leaned near the sleeping body of the man and the dark fall of her hair came over him. She hesitated, touched him lightly with a finger, lifted her head and howled softly. The cavern walls howled very softly back.

The Yunggamurra rose and went quickly to the farthest corner of the cavern and crouched inside the dark fall of her hair. She waited and listened still but she did not go near the man or look at him again.

4

Wirrun stood in the cave of death and breathed air with the burnt-honey sweetness of gum-blossom. The lost white bones of the dead were pitiful yet they had strength; disjointed fingers lying here had painted those dark eyes in the outer cavern. He felt tall and strong, not smoke-drifting or dream-seeing like a man in sleep but more fully alive than he had ever felt, and he strode towards the inner cave of Wulgaru.

It was good to move so surely over the uneven rock. He went into the firelight and found Wulgaru sitting where he had sat before with the Moomba around him. When they saw him they laughed aloud and thronged about him rubbing their hands over their own bodies and his, exchanging sweat in the business of friendship. He felt no awe or triumph but stood looking over their heads at the great tree-trunk body and mask-face of Wulgaru. It spoke to him graciously.

"I welcome you, Man, great-grandson of my maker. Sit by my fire and talk to me."

The Moomba laughing and nodding moved aside but Wirrun still stood and looked at Wulgaru; and again he was filled with a sort of pity. For this was another puppet, more clumsily made but with strength and not yet broken. He saw that truly it took its power from men; it had none but what they gave it, no wisdom but what they taught it, and in evil or good was only obedient to them.

"You've not destroyed me, then," he said.

The mask smiled and the eyes burnt white like the terrible stars. "I have not destroyed you with fear or your own evil. I have not destroyed you like another man."

"We had a bargain," said Wirrun.

"It was made good when you sent the eastern ghost home."

"That's reasons and argument. I don't trust to them." He laid his hand on the shape of the stone. "I kept my word and never used this against you, but now it's over I got the right again. I speak for the powers of the land and I order you and yours to keep your own country from now on for all the time there is."

"You may order without the stone or the land's old beetles. Do you not also thank me?" Wirrun was silent. "There have been Clever Men," said Wulgaru, "who thanked me for their making."

Wirrun smiled. "If I'm Clever I was born that way. No thanks to you." For he would not teach the creature any more power.

The eyes blazed white again but the voice said only, "You say true. Go, then, and find out who you are and where is home. I fear I shall not see you soon."

Wirrun gave one nod of farewell to Wulgaru and one to the Moomba and turned to go. Behind him the tree-voice murmured wistfully.

"Yet I think you may thank me."

Wirrun did not look back. He did not look again at the small lost bones in the second cave or, since he did not have the marks, at the paintings in the first. He strode light and easy out of the cave into country he knew, under the edge of the escarpment.

It was bright with the day's last sun and fell steeply away to wide grasslands and scrub. He could see the mouth of the valley where the river ran in between outlying arms of the escarpment to his camp. That other dreary plain was gone, the plain where the crowd of the dead had danced and he had fought with Wulgaru—yet when he thought of it it was there for a moment, shimmering at the edges like vanishing desert water.

He climbed strongly into the air and travelled over the known country. He wanted to shout with the power and fullness of living, with joy that his work was done and his battle over. He wanted to see the Yunggamurra's eyes turn to moonlight and to hear her sing a song of heroes. And before he crept back into his puppet body and put his flesh between them—before he went away at last and left her safe and free—they would look at each other again. They would know that in spite of all laws and all time they loved each other and were truly man and wife.

With the speed of spirits he came over the hill, found the tree and the pot-hole and slid into the cavern. It seemed to be empty but he knew she was there and shouted impatiently.

"Water-girl! Come out of that! Where are you?"

She came glimmering out of the dark and stood with hands folded and head bent. "I am here, Great One."

He laughed enormously. "You knew, then? You saw? It was just like you said only worse! I was scared right through. Oh, girl!" He stretched till he seemed to fill the cave and still she stood with bent head, and he laughed again at her pretended respect and thought how small and fragile she was and how lovely. "I'm starving," he boasted. "Any more of those cakes left?"

She looked up very gravely. "You are hungry?"

"I could eat a horse."

"The dead," she said, "are never hungry."

He frowned.

"You travelled fast and well?" she asked earnestly. "Was the sun warm? You heard the birds and smelled the honey?"

"What's wrong, girl?" he asked. Her eyes were dark. Without knowing he did it he took her hands in his. "Don't be scared. Everything's fine. Tell me what's up."

"See!" she cried. "You breathe deep! Your hands are strong and warm."

"Yours too. What's up?"

She swung away behind her hair. "You cannot trust the Yunggamurra! You have won and I have failed! Go and see."

He tried to draw her with him but she pulled back; so he went alone to the corner with the bed of grass and looked down at Wirrun sleeping. And he saw he was turned into stone.

"So the Big Cap won after all," he said dazedly. "He's destroyed me." But he knew it was not so. Even this moment of shock could not blunt his freed mind; he knew he had been changed as ancestors and heroes and lesser men before him had been changed. The land was silently peopled with them; among its ancient rocks their stone bodies lay in warning or in promise while they themselves lived on; behind the wind as the old men said. Now he too lived behind the wind. He had grown out of now into forever.

But he felt a great tearing pang that he had lost the companionship of men, and of desolation that he was free and homeless, a being without a place. And behind him, as if in answer to that, he heard the Yunggamurra sobbing. He turned away from the blurred and coarsened shape of himself and went to her, where she sat weeping within the dark fall of her hair.

He sat near and drew her against his shoulder as he would have done once, and laid his cheek on her hair. "Now then, girl," he said gently teasing, "you never did that. I got a lot of faith in you but this was something bigger. Nothing you could help. Bigger than you and Wulgaru both."

She went on sobbing.

"Come on, now. Some people'd be *glad* if a friend of theirs got turned into a hero forever."

"But you did not choose it!" she cried. "You have lost your old self and you set me to watch!"

"And you went off playing with the wind and singing to the grass, *I* know, and when you got back there was this red-eyed thing turning me into a rock. Well I'll just have to beat you, I reckon. A man's gotta beat his wife now and then."

The Yunggamura gave another sob or two and fell silent. Wirrun was silent too; the silence lengthened. There was only the rustle of water over rock, and some fragment that fell into it with a small clear *plink!* of surprise. When they had both listened for some time to Wirrun's last words he lifted his head and laughed again; not largely this time but deep and quiet.

"I gotta hand it to him," he said. "He did win. And I shoulda thanked him. Girl dear, do you think your sisters'd steal his wife from a proper forever sort of hero?"

She smiled a secret Yunggamurra smile in the darkness of her hair. "Surely," she said, "he would spring up into the storm and take her back?"

"And beat 'em off with whips of lightning. Or follow them to their only river and call her out of it. That's if she was the right sort, one that'd come with him. She'd have to be the sort that broke free on her own and got turned a bit by the sun. A gold Yunggamurra."

"Surely," she said peeping wickedly, "a proper hero would take no other sort? For a man must take the Yunggamurra he can catch but a Great One may choose."

"Is that what the law says?"

"The law of the Yunggamurra is for men and not for Great Ones."

"Well," said Wirrun, "I don't know how great but I travel very fast on air. And I could still eat a horse only you don't like horse. Will we go east to the sea-tainted water and catch a fish for breakfast?"

She considered gravely. "May we cook it on a fire?"

"Dear girl! But here's your own place, with your own river and all. If you leave it something might steal it from you."

She lifted her chin with the old fierce pride. "Nothing would dare. Have you no place in the east, and would you lose it?"

"When a man claims all countries home's everywhere."

"Then let us go east and find the morning and ride it west! There are rivers and hills and forests to see again."

"And winds and waterfalls to ride."

"And strange old things to peep at, and stones that grow and sparkle in dark places!"

"But I tell you I'm hungry, girl—"

"That is not important. If there are no fish there will be turtle-eggs or a rabbit."

So the hero and the water-girl went from the cavern up into the green evening sky; and a shy stooped figure, that had seen one of them turned gold and the other to stone, nodded gently and watched them go. But where they went only the land knew.

In time, as word spread down the long roads, most of the Ice-Fighter's story was put together and told; but its ending changed from place to place and often it only drifted into silence. For in the Centre, and in the high country under the Cape, and below the great northern escarpment, there were men who claimed that the story was not ended and the Ice-Fighter was still around. He had been seen, they said, sitting at a campfire in the evening and talking with a friend—but when a stranger came near he went away quickly, and the man who was left at the fire only shook his head and would say nothing.

The old south land lies like an open hand under the stars. They shine more brightly there. They tell their stories to every kind of man and the stories change from country to country. So one group is the Southern Cross here, and there a black swan flying from a spear; another is Orion's Belt, or again it is the sisters of the eagle. But one group keeps its name through many stories: it is called the Seven Sisters.

Under the escarpment these seven are the Yunggamurra. They were human once, sisters who broke the law and were changed in punishment; the cruel and lovely and vanishing singers of the river. The stars too are veiled in shifting darkness like the Yunggamurra in their hair. They gleam and vanish as the sisters do and are very hard to count. Few men see that now there are only six.

The seventh Yunggamurra has broken free and roams the land with Wirrun.

ABOUT THE AUTHOR

Patricia Wrightson was born and brought up in New South Wales, and for some years she edited the *School Magazine* produced by the New South Wales Department of Education. She has two grown-up children, and now lives on the banks of the River Clarence.

Patricia Wrightson is acknowledged as one of today's greatest writers for children. Her first book, *The Crooked Snake*, won the Children's Book Council (Australian) Award in 1956. *'I Own the Racecourse!'* was runner up for the Children's Book of the Year Award in Australia in 1970, an award which Patricia Wrightson won with *The Nargun and the Stars* in 1974 and *The Ice is Coming* in 1978. *'I Own the Racecourse!'* and *The Nargun and the Stars* were also included in the Hans Christian Andersen Honours list, in 1970 and 1976, and *The Ice is Coming* was honours listed for the *Guardian* Award in 1978.

In the 1978 New Year Honours List Patricia Wrightson was awarded the O.B.E. for her services to literature.

Other titles in the Puffin Plus series

THE ICE IS COMING
Patricia Wrightson

Wirrun was a man of the People, who had lived in the
land since the Dreamtime. He was young and educated
in the ways of the whites. But when the mountain cried
for help, he heard. For the Ninya, the ancient ice-spirits,
were seeking to bring a new ice age to the land.
Together with the Mimi, a rock-spirit from far away,
Wirrun set out to find the Eldest Nargun, a creature
of living rock that had defeated the Ninya in the long-
gone past. And with the Power given him by a hero-
spirit, he could see and command all the ancient
earth-spirits. But the way was long and hard – and the
eldest Nargun was not what he expected . . .

The first in the trilogy, *The Book of Wirrun.*

THE DARK BRIGHT WATER
Patricia Wrightson

Far down in the dark caverns the river-spirit howled and sang her siren song. And across the land the earth-spirits fled, while the People watched in despair as the vital waters dried up or changed courses. Their call went out to Wirrun, the Hero who had saved them once before with the magic power he carried. But Wirrun was haunted and driven by the song of the Yungamurra. While he quested without answer to find the trouble of the land, the lure of the singing drew him inexorably toward the old, dark waters where the women with tails waited and taunted the spirit they had caught.

The second in the trilogy, *The Book of Wirrun*.

DISPLACED PERSON
Lee Harding

The streets are leached of colour; rush-hour crowds bustle soundlessly. People seem to be oblivious of his presence. Graeme Drury's world is slipping away from him – or has he slipped out of it? The grey confusion encroaches, isolating him somewhere beyond reality. But if this is not reality, what of the old tramp and the green-eyed girl?

Displaced Person is the winner of two Australian awards.

THE BOY WHO SAW GOD
Ted Greenwood

All his life Leo had lived behind or above shops. Mostly milk bars and newsagencies like the one in the small township of Manoora, where he had just moved with his mother and Rick.

Leo tried hard not to hate Rick, his mother's friend. His mother had told him that being with Rick made things easier for her. Leo couldn't understand why – Rick was awful to her, and deliberately made life difficult for him.

Then when Leo believes that God has ordered him to sacrifice a sheep, little does he realize the consequences his action will have . . .

WHAT ABOUT TOMORROW
Ivan Southall

Sam's nightmare begins when, riding a bike without brakes, he loses control and crashes headlong into a tram. His life suddenly changes – 'You're nothing now, Sam,' he told himself.

As Sam's life unfolds, the present, the past and the future become entwined in a stream of events. He treads a stony path to maturity and self-discovery, helped towards his tomorrow by three girls and other friends. But the boy who becomes a man has to face another moment of terror in a Sunderland flying boat, diving to the attack.

FLY WEST
Ivan Southall

It was said, during the Second World War, that Britain could die in the Atlantic, for without the convoys carrying food, weapons and men from America, she could never have survived. It was the convoys that formed the Atlantic bridge that kept her alive. If Hitler could break the bridge, Britain was his for the taking. But first of all he had to get his U-boats out past Norway in the north, and France in the south, and over each lane sat the Sunderlands of Coastal Command, keeping the U-boats penned in.

This is Ivan Southall's personal account of the men who flew the incredible Sunderland flying boat – 'the flying porcupine' – into battle over the Atlantic. They were not the conventional heroes – they were bent on staying alive – and this is their story from the inside.

EMPTY WORLD
John Christopher

When a deadly virus sweeps the world, gathering in intensity until it seems that the world is indeed empty, how can Neil cope with the necessities of life as well as the more subtle pressures of fear and loneliness?

THE DEVIL ON THE ROAD
Robert Westall

John Webster took no chances with his Triumph Tiger-Cub, but he thought he played games with Chance, like tossing a coin to see which road to follow. But maybe Chance was playing games with him?

WHY DIDN'T THEY TELL THE HORSES?
Christine McKenna

Actress Christine McKenna had never been on a horse in her life (apart from an endearing donkey on the sands at the age of three). So when she landed the star role of the hunting and riding Christina in the TV serial, *Flambards*, some incredible experiences were ahead of her. This is the good-natured, frequently hilarious story of her relationship with a host of horses . . .

MURPHY'S MOB
Michael Saunders

Dunmore United's run-down ground is the haunt of all the local tearaways – kids like Gerry, Boxer and Wurzel. So when the new manager, Mac Murphy, lets them form their own Supporters Club, everyone thinks he's crazy. But Murphy's Mob are determined to prove him right. Recently serialized on TV.

A MIDSUMMER NIGHT'S DEATH
K. M. Peyton

When the body of the unpopular English master, Mr Robinson, was taken from the river, Jonathan didn't feel very involved in the tragedy. But then he realized another master, one he really liked, had lied to the police – and soon he began to doubt whether the coroner's verdict of suicide had been the right one.

NOAH'S CASTLE
John Rowe Townsend

Set in a lawless, hungry Britain, this provocative work paints a chilling picture of a family under stress, revealing their weaknesses and their strengths.

THE INTRUDER
John Rowe Townsend

When 16-year-old Arnold Haithwaite is asked to guide a stranger across miles of dangerous sands, he finds his life suddenly threatened. This story with its wild setting was made into an award-winning TV serial.

A LONG WAY TO GO
Marjorie Darke

The fighting rages in France, and posters all over London demand that young men should join up. But Luke has other feelings – feelings that are bound to bring great trouble on him and the family. Because nobody has much sympathy for a conscientious objector. Perhaps the only answer is to go on the run? A fascinating and unusual story of one young man's attempt to stick out for what he believes is right.

THE ENNEAD
Jan Mark

A vivid and compelling story about Euterpe, the third planet in a system of nine known as the Ennead, where scheming and bribery are needed to survive.

THE GHOST ON THE HILL
John Gordon

An eerie story which shows the author's ability both to portray delicate relationships and also to evoke a chilling sense of the unknown.

THE TWELFTH DAY OF JULY
ACROSS THE BARRICADES
INTO EXILE
A PROPER PLACE
HOSTAGES TO FORTUNE
Joan Lingard

A series of novels about modern Belfast which highlight the problems of the troubles there, in the story of Protestant Sadi and Catholic Kevin which even an 'escape' to England fails to solve.

MISCHLING, SECOND DEGREE
Ilse Koehn

Ilse was a 'Mischling', a child of mixed race, a dangerous birthright in Nazi Germany. The perils of an outsider in the Hitler Youth and in military girls' camps make this a vivid and fascinating true story.

ONE MORE RIVER
Lynne Reid Banks

The conflict of personal and political loyalties explored through the friendship of a Jewish girl with an Arab boy.

TULKU
Peter Dickinson

Escape from massacre, journey through bandit lands, encounters with strange Tibetan powers – and beneath the adventures are layers of idea and insight. Winner of both the Carnegie and Whitbread Awards for 1979.

SURVIVAL
Russell Evans

High tension adventure of a Russian political prisoner on the run in the midst of an Arctic winter.

A QUEST FOR ORION
Rosemary Harris

Europe overrun by neo-Stalinists is the setting for this compelling depiction of resistance to tyranny and of the improvisation and endurance needed in a fragmented world.

More about Penguins and Pelicans

For further information about books available from Penguin please write to Dept EP, Penguin Books Ltd, Harmondsworth, Middlesex UB7 ODA.

In the U.S.A.: For a complete list of books available from Penguin in the United States write to Dept DG, Penguin Books, 299 Murray Hill Parkway, East Rutherford, New Jersey 07073.

In Canada: For a complete list of books available from Penguin in Canada write to Penguin Books Canada Ltd, 2801 John Street, Markham, Ontario L3R 1B4.

In Australia: For a complete list of books available from Penguin in Australia write to the Marketing Department, Penguin Books Australia Ltd, P.O. Box 257, Ringwood, Victoria 3134.

In New Zealand: For a complete list of books available from Penguin in New Zealand write to the Marketing Department, Penguin Books (N.Z.) Ltd, P.O. Box 4019, Auckland 10.